MW00941457

Geoffrey P. Ward's

Guide

to

Villainy

M.A. Nichols

Copyright © 2017 by M.A. Nichols

All rights reserved. No part of this publication may be reproduced or transmitted, in any form or by any means, electronic, mechanical, photocopying, recording, or otherwise, without the prior permission of the copyright owner.

The characters and events portrayed in this book are fictitious. Any similarity to real persons, living or dead, is coincidental and not intended by the author.

www.ma-nichols.com

To those
tenacious and patient
enough to fight
for their dreams

Table of Contents

A Word Before We Start

I would rather jump right to the point—it is the reason you picked up this book in the first place—but I feel it necessary to explain a bit about myself and the purpose of this guide, so bear with me. My name is Geoffrey P. Ward. While most authors would give a long-winded introduction explaining the intricate details of their life leading them to publish their book, including shining an inordinately bright light on how qualified they are to expound on the subject, I will keep it brief.

As to my non-professional history, you don't care where I came from or who my family is. While they played a role in how I fell into this profession, it doesn't matter in the context of this guide. Professionally speaking, I started at the age of eighteen and have roughly seventeen years of experience working as a villainy consultant. After being offered my first consulting job, I worked mainly with faeries, stepmothers, fiefdoms, and the odd minor kingdom. Since then, I've grown into the most sought after villainy consultant in all the land. Granted, I am the only villainy consultant in all the land, but I provide a valuable service nonetheless.

There is an extreme lack of resources for villains. Princes have wizards, mages, or captains of the guard training them from birth. Farm boys have their grizzled hermits to guide them. Princesses and exceptionally comely peasant girls have fairy godmothers and a myriad of magical creatures popping into their lives at prime dramatic intervals. Villains have no one.

The odds are stacked against us.

And in case you missed that, yes, I count myself a villain. No, I haven't conquered a kingdom or destroyed the lives of others. At least, none that didn't deserve it. But as I've been told by countless non-villains, the nature of my job plants me firmly in the villain camp.

My services provide crucial guidance and information to the aspiring villain, which help mold them into the success they wish to be. However, I've reached the point where my schedule is far more limited than the number of applicants petitioning for my services, so I thought it best to write down the most common advice I give my clients to help those unable to have me personally in their corner.

Regardless of the reasons why you are starting this path, your success relies on help and knowledge. While my help is limited (this is a guide book, not a spell book, after all), I have the knowledge in spades. This guide will outline valuable principles to help you achieve success and survive long enough to enjoy it.

The Black, the White, and Everything Between

Before delving into how to succeed as a villain, it is important that we spend a moment on what it means to be one. No doubt, you have an idea in your head, but that image is the product of stories that paint heroes as the strong arm of the righteous, damsels in distress as angels, and villains as demon spawn. The truth of it is much more complex than the stark categorization non-villains would have you believe.

Let me tell you a little story:

Once upon a time, there was a man who wanted to make more of his life than he had been given at birth. He worked hard to climb the ladder of success only to be kicked down and stepped on by anyone higher than him. No matter what he did, he couldn't improve his situation because a small minority held the power and only allowed those of their choosing to succeed. Anyone else was put in their place. So, the man did what any ambitious self-starter should do. He wrestled the power away from those setting the status quo and through his own labors, grabbed what he wanted from life. And he lived happily ever after.

This is a story I've heard repeatedly. Most villains are

simply building a life beyond what destiny or magic doles out. Non-villains expect you to accept your lot for what it is and never step higher.

"You're born this way, and you'll die this way," they say, never giving a single thought as to why that is. If you're born a peddler's child, you'll either become a peddler or marry a peddler. To desire more leaves you with only two options: disappointment or villainy.

Our fellow in the story didn't lack drive, ambition, or ability, all of which should lead to better things. But to non-villains, the world is written in stone and cannot be changed; there are roles each of us plays and stepping outside that is wicked. There are the royals and the peasants, and never the twain shall meet. Except when it comes to taxes.

At this point, you may be thinking of stories refuting that statement—some peasant girl who married a prince or the farm boy that went off on grand adventures, receiving boatloads of glory and a princess to marry—but those are only the exceptions. Magic allows variations to the rigid order, but fairy godmothers are selective in choosing those worthy of magical intervention, giving it only to those who have the right combination of poverty and attractiveness. If you're poor and gorgeous, good things may be coming your way. All others need not apply.

Being a hero is an exclusive club. They have strict rules about who is and isn't allowed in, and those operating outside those dictates are labeled a villain. But villains are those who would rather rely on skill and hard work than nature or fairy godmothers. It is not our deeds that earn us that label, but the arbitrary dictates of the heroes.

The line between hero and villain is clearly defined by heroes, but the moral implications of heroism versus villainy is hazy. There are villains who never do anything objectively evil, but by choosing their own path, they're vilified. In fact, the most successful villains are those who would be considered heroic if their father had been a woodsman or a king instead of an accountant, or if a wizard or fairy godmother helped them instead of me.

Wanting to be in charge is not inherently villainous. Kings and the rest of the royal foppery are nothing more than beneficiaries of an accident of birth. Their character and ability to lead never factor into whether they deserve their status and power, yet they are called noble. However, when a person proves they are capable of leading despite not having the right social standing, they're called villains. They're considered evil, malicious, and conniving. But having brains and drive is not a malevolent thing, and upsetting the status quo is not vile.

If you choose villainy, people will try to stop you. Using every ounce of wit and logic, they will try to convince you to give up. If that does not work, they will enlist any prince or pre-destined peasant they can wrangle to use brute force to maintain the ever-worshipped status quo. They will destroy everything you build, and they are the "heroes".

The general bias against rule breakers isn't helped by the unreliability of the stories we hear. When a hero and villain square off, the only one to know the full truth is the one who walks away victorious. In turn, that truth is skewed by the victor to fit whatever reality they wish to portray to the public. The heroes get painted more heroic and the villains more villainous, regardless of the truth.

A stepmother is dubbed "wicked" by her stepdaughter simply because the woman cares more about her natural born daughters. When that stepdaughter swoops in and steals that life of luxury her stepmother has built, she not only gets the prize but the ability to tell the tale of her stepfamily's tortures, thus cementing the stepmother's "wicked" label. Never mind that the woman generally isn't around to defend herself against the slander.

To the victor go the spoils, and one of the greatest is the ability to paint the past in whatever colors you choose. In some cases, even villains can claim hero-hood if they are successful in defeating their foe. Though I don't see the point. Embrace your villainous nature. It's only a label.

Villains and evil are not synonymous, nor are they mutually exclusive. Rather, they are too often mistaken for each other. Evil is malicious and violent, but villainy is ending up on the wrong side of an argument. If you wish for any level of success in your villainous endeavors, you must accept that the tales you heard while bouncing on your mother's knee may not be accurate.

Disclaimers

1. The majority of my clients fall into the large-scale villain category, meaning they have their sights set on dominating a kingdom or even the world, so the bulk of this guide will be centered on them. But these princi- ples apply to anyone with villainous intent—from the High Lord of the Realm to the lowly stepmother. This guide is here to help all those taking the difficult path

of villainy.

2. I hope you find this guide useful, but if you don't, you've already bought the book so it no longer matters to me. Don't bother contacting me to argue about my advice. I stand by what is written here, and if you disagree, I don't care. And if you're one of those busy-bodies looking for evidence with which to tear apart me and my company, don't bother. I don't care if you agree with me or not. I've been called worse names than you can possibly imagine by people I care about far more than you.

3. Except my own name, all others have been changed to protect the confidentiality of my clients and to protect myself from the spiteful retaliation of the "innocent" who may not be portrayed here as heroically as they have hitherto claimed. I've been in this business long enough to know how to mitigate trouble with such people, but avoiding it is always the better option.

Chapter One

All Villains are Not Created Equal

O nce you step onto this path, you'll find there are many ways to traverse it. Villainy is more than buying black leather ensembles and kidnapping fair maidens. Outside the villainy industry, most assume all villains are the same, which is quite idiotic when you think of it, but heroes aren't known for their intellectual depth (the boring dolts).

Your success is dependent on deciding early in your career what type of villain you wish to be. Each has their strengths and shortcomings, along with issues specific to their role. The more understanding you have of your villainy type, the better your chance of success.

The Overlord

As the name implies, this is the villain who wants to take over. Whether it's a family unit or a kingdom, the Overlord wants not only to be in charge but to have a giant spotlight shining on them while their underlings bask in their glory. They don't want any confusion about who's alpha. When people think villain, it's generally the Overlord that pops into their head because it is the most obvious and public type.

But don't let the name fool you. An Overlord may take power with the sword or subtlety. Don't assume that you have to do it with an army. The most effective Overlords I've worked with use subterfuge to gain their end goal. The fewer people you anger in your rise to power, the fewer repercussions.

I worked with a young lady by the name of Frederica who had high political aspirations without the political and social capital to make it work the heroic way. Raised among the landed gentry, she grew up familiar with the upper echelons of society, but not being a member of the royal elite, she had no hope of breaking that barrier.

While marriage alliances are common for men and women to better their position, the marriage game is usually only played by royalty or people of higher rank and position than Frederica. She could have married well, but she had her eyes on a bigger prize. She was stuck in the heroic wasteland—too poor to buy her way in and too rich to attract magical help. Luckily, there was a kingdom not far from her home with a future king in need of a bride.

Frankly, the guy had the unfortunate combination of being neither good looking nor bright; most princes are handsome enough to make up for their lack of intelligence. Regardless, this prince was determined to find a bride. After all, a title can make up for both, even if you're sprinting past your youth into middle age and have more hair coming from your nose than your scalp.

Princesses flocked to the kingdom, hoping to be picked, but each was rejected. Frederica and I discovered the prince's mother had twisted requirements to find that proper bride for her son. Being a princess wasn't enough. The queen wanted a "true princess" for a daughter-in-law. To this day, I have no idea what she meant by that, since the only requirement to be a princess is being born into the right family. But to prove the princess's trueness, the queen gave each girl a test. After years of searching, the prince was still a swinging and aging bachelor.

The queen and her son caused such a ruckus among the various royal families that discovering the nature of the tests was easy enough. Besides being a perfect physical specimen of womanhood, the princess had to exemplify impeccable deportment and decorum. And feel a pea under a mountain of mattresses. Why anyone would want someone that pathetically frail, I have no idea, but the queen claimed it showed the girl's delicate nature. I suspect it had more to do with the queen not wanting to relinquish her title or role in the kingdom to her daughter-in-law. I asked her about it years ago, and she denied any impropriety, but I'm not convinced.

The rest was easy. I thought it would be more difficult

to get the attention of the prince, but Frederica showed up on his doorstep one rainy night and told everyone she was a princess. I think the prince was getting a bit desperate at this point. He was close to forty, single, and still living under his mother's thumb. The prince insisted she be tested, so his mother agreed. Frederica awoke the next morning with pea-sized bruises painted on her back and sides, forcing the queen to capitulate. Frederica and the prince were married three days later.

This may sound like a strange way to be an Overlord, but Frederica's story couldn't have ended better. By the time her husband discovered the scam, they'd ascended the throne and Frederica was firmly ensconced as ruler. The minute they were crowned, she'd wrestled control away from her husband and turned around their mismanaged kingdom, proving to his people and supporters that she was a far better ruler. Rather than return to the way things were, everyone (including the newly crowned king) agreed to turn a blind eye.

After sending her mother-in-law to spend her retirement years tucked away in some remote part of the country, Frederica has successfully reigned the kingdom for several years. Frederica got the crown, the power, and the goodies that go with it. She does spend her life with an imbecile by her side, but she is a successful ruler of a now prosperous kingdom, and no one has overthrown her. This would not have happened without subtlety, patience, and a great deal of skill.

Though patience isn't required to get your prize, it is for keeping it. Taking power too aggressively results in a huge amount of social upset, which generally shakes loose a few hopeful heroes, one of whom is bound to overthrow your plans. You must understand that the more attention you draw, the higher chance a hero will notice and decide to stop you.

The only time that doesn't happen is when you're so subtle in your machinations that those in power don't realize what you've done until it's too late. Or not at all. For Frederica, by the time they figured it out, she had firmly entrenched herself in the role of queen, creating herself as the new status quo. The dowager queen and the king may have wanted to oust her, but everyone else had adjusted to the change and didn't want to go back to the way it was. Frederica was a good queen, and to remove her would have made too much of a fuss.

While many of my Overlord clients tend to fail eventually, those who are careful and crafty not only survive their reign but thrive. For the record, that failure usually comes from refusing to implement some pertinent piece of advice I gave them. Just putting that out there.

If you struggle with self-control or get fixated on distractions, Overlord isn't the right fit for you. Period. I've seen it too many times. You must be focused and willing to listen when advisors warn you. I'm not saying that just because I make my living as a contracted advisor. If you can't be humble enough to listen when they're advising you to abandon your plans of marrying the unwilling princess or to ignore the young upstart and his grizzled companion who are causing relatively minor problems, you will never succeed as an Overlord.

Done right, the Overlord isn't a bad path to take, but it's not for the faint of heart or the foolhardy. The Overlord climbs the highest but often falls the hardest.

The Counselor

Less well known, but far more successful is the Counselor. It is very similar to the Overlord in that power and dominance are their core villainous motivations. They are both leaders and rulers with one difference—the Overlord wants the spotlight, the Counselor doesn't. The Counselor is content to be the power behind the throne. They allow someone else to be in the public eye, preferring to be the figurehead's puppet master. Though not a single other person may realize it, the Counselor is the one truly in charge, making all the monkeys dance to the Counselor's tune.

Both the Counselor and the Overlord are long-standing villains. Where other villains can leave the area once they've completed their mission making it easier to survive, the Counselor and the Overlord only reach the end of their villainy journey when they're ready to retire. Since their goal is to hold the reins of the group they rule, there's not a clear endpoint.

Being front and center, this is more an issue for the Overlord than the Counselor. The more attention you garner, the more likely you'll attract heroes, but the Counselor works in the shadows and has a much higher survival rate. If people overlook you, they won't see your knife until it's firmly planted in their back. Okay, so that was a bit gruesome, but the metaphor illustrates my point.

If you have any desire to stand in the spotlight, you will not survive in this role. Many villains want some level of recognition, but seeking accolades often leads to failure and a horribly painful death when your monkeys turn on you. For the Counselor, it is imperative to allow the recognized rulers to believe they are making the decisions. The minute they realize they're being manipulated, they will get rid of you.

Besides needing to be humble enough to allow others to take the glory, the Counselor villain must have excellent people skills. Manipulation is their main tool of the trade. Generally, this is a skill that you must be born with. It can be honed, but it's very difficult to develop. Not impossible, but difficult.

Due to the nature of the job, the Counselor has the highest degree of uncertainty. Done correctly, it has a low mortality rate, but by its nature, it's dependent on others working with you. Non-villains working with you, to be precise. Your fate is tied to the person or people you're manipulating. Circumstances can change rapidly when your success rests on someone else holding the power. While the truly gifted can make it work regardless of what happens, it can be very tricky to bet on the right horse. Thus, the Counselor must be flexible, adaptable, and highly intelligent.

One of my clients suffered from the condition of having high ambitions with not enough nobility in his blood to achieve it. Much like Frederica, Charles was born to a good family. High enough to be taunted by the upper crust, but too low to enter their prestigious ranks. Too rich for magical help, and too poor for royal acceptance.

What he did have was a beautiful daughter.

Beautiful daughters are an invaluable commodity to Counselors. That may sound heartless, but the fact is that if you have one, she can attract princes and kings by the barrelful in the right circumstances. Especially if she is a kind-hearted doormat or not particularly bright. The first big hurdle for a Counselor is getting into the good graces of someone in power, and being his father-in-law is a great boon. Especially when most princes who marry gorgeous but vapid girls are generally vapid themselves and much easier to manipulate. Charles understood this and knew his daughter was his best chance for success.

However, in her current circumstances, Charles' daughter wouldn't meet anyone of importance. Too lowly for royal notice, her best bet was to gain magical sympathy, but her station was still too high to attract it. His daughter needed a steep decline in prosperity, but in a manner that wouldn't land him in trouble.

Charles' wife had died years before, so he looked to the marriage arena for the answer to his problem. Finding a most obnoxious woman with two equally obnoxious daughters of her own, Charles snatched them up and brought them home. It was a perfect situation.

Other than having to deal with his new wife for a few weeks—just long enough to convince his daughter that he was besotted—he left for "business" in a neighboring kingdom whereupon he met with an "accident". Feigning amnesia, Charles pretended to forget his former life, allowing him to disappear from his daughter's life and leaving her to the machinations of her stepmother.

You see, heroes and heroines are entirely too gullible when it comes to amnesia. This has been a bit overused, so it's not foolproof, but in this instance it was the perfect move. Plausible deniability is a powerful tool for any villain, but most especially the Counselor. Being able to claim you don't remember the things you've done or having an excuse for an extended absence is absolute gold. Charles was able to let nature take its course and swoop in when things resolved to his liking.

Neither Charles nor I have been able to get all the details about what happened because his silly daughter either can't remember the details or is the world's worst liar (my money is on the first). Either way, each time she tells the story, it changes. I've heard at least three wildly different tales and a dozen more variations on those, so I'm not entirely clear on the specifics, but I've pieced together some common threads.

Charles's second wife, the "wicked" stepmother, turned out as horrible as he hoped she would be. She and her equally unlikable daughters immediately turned their attentions to tormenting their pretty rival. It sounds like it mostly involved them having her do a lot of chores around the house, but the way the girl tells it, you'd think she'd been tortured. She could have just refused to do it, but Charles' daughter was always a bit spineless.

One day there was some grand announcement that the prince was throwing a Bride Finding Ball. If you've not heard of it, the big ol' BFB is exactly what it sounds like.

Some royal decides they want to get married, throws a big party, and chooses from the eligible ladies. Personally, I'd want a more solid foundation for a lifelong commitment than a few dances and a couple minutes of conversation, but royals prefer courtship quick and with little communication between the two parties. It's further proof that higher ups tend to care more about appearance than substance.

Charles' daughter wanted to go, but the wicked stepmother didn't want to allow someone there who would outshine her own daughters. She forbade the girl to go and took away all her BFB-ready dresses, so she didn't have anything to wear.

Apparently, months of servitude weren't enough for the girl to throw up too much of a fuss, but this was the breaking point. What comes next is the haziest aspect of the story. Some claim a fairy godmother appeared, some claim talking birds, others say it was an anthropomorphic tree. Again, Charles' daughter isn't the quickest of creatures, and the whole story has gotten muddled.

Regardless, what is clear is that when she cried, magic came to save the day. Magic can't stop itself from swooping in when a beautiful girl is being persecuted. Even more so when she's crying. Most magic creatures on the side of "good" have told me that they like to bestow kindness on those who are kind and have fallen on hard times, brushing off the fact that those kind people always seem to be the embodiment of beauty. I think they're unable to look past the surface; they can't tell the difference between passivity or good looks and goodness. Most of the girls I see helped are in dire straits because they are passive twits, not put-upon angels.

Charles' daughter got to the BFB, and life was good. She met the prince, entrancing His Royal Vapidness with her stunning good looks. Even if she wasn't good at telling time. Most magical creatures love a dramatic twist and help their charges with extreme caveats destined to cause some issues, and in this case, the magic helping her ran out at the stroke of midnight. She lost track of time and barely got out of the ballroom before the prince saw her rich clothes turn into rags. As a side note, being afraid your intended won't accept you if you're not wearing fancy clothes is not a great sign of future success in your marriage.

And this is where the story gets a bit strange. It's one of the few details that remains constant in each retelling, so I suppose it's likely to be true—regardless of how ridiculous. During her flight, she lost her shoe, which the prince found. Rather than simply searching the area for the woman who looked like the girl he fell in "love" with at the BFB, he used the shoe. In his mind, only the right girl would fit it, so he had every lady in the kingdom try it on. Now, I'm not germophobic, but it would take a lot of enticing for me to put on a shoe that had been worn by every other person in the kingdom. Trust me, you do not want to know about the outbreak of warts that swept the kingdom.

Upon finding the right foot, the prince married Charles' daughter, and I'd like to say they lived happily ever after, but they lived as happily ever after as possible for two people who knew nothing about the other before marrying.

Either way, Charles showed up on their doorstep

shortly after their marriage using his now cured amnesia as an excuse for not arriving sooner to save his daughter from her wicked stepmother. All was forgiven, and he moved right in with them. It's the best situation he could have hoped for. His daughter married well, throwing him into another sphere of influence and power. His son-in-law is easy to manipulate; the kid couldn't identify his future bride without her trying on the shoe first, and in some stories I've heard, he needed an extra dose of magic to step in and keep him from marrying the wrong girls who realized that fitting into a small shoe required only the slice of a knife. On top of that, Charles's second wife and stepdaughters took the blame.

Consequently, the wicked stepmother and her daughters suffered a gruesome death. Most heroines may appear to be sweet and good-natured, but do not cross them and get caught because you will suffer worse at their hand than from a hero's. I heard the girl once claim that she forgave their wickedness and another time she said she arranged for her stepsisters to be married to lords or some such nonsense, but I know for a fact that she had the stepmother's and stepsisters' eyes pecked out by rabid birds. Ick.

Such is the inequality between the heroes and the villains. I'm not saying those three weren't miserable human beings, but being pecked to death in retribution for servitude is a bit of an overreaction. It was a much harsher punishment than Charles or I expected them to receive.

But this is beside the point. Charles got what he wanted. Though to the world, it looks as though the prince (now king) rules his country with his blushing bride at his side, it's Charles who pulls the strings. No one is the wiser, and all three parties are happy. The girl got her handsome prince, the prince got an advisor who can make the hard decisions for him, and Charles got the power and position he craved. Win, win, win.

Except for the stepmother and her daughters.

The Punisher

Wanting to right a wrong is a common motivator for villains, and that is at the heart and soul of a Punisher. Whether it's avenging or seeking justice, the Punisher wants to balance the cosmic scales of right and wrong.

In general, villains are a volatile lot, and during the course of your life you will meet people who need a bit of punishing; whether getting beaten up during your adolescence or losing the love of your life to some bozo who spends more time in front of the looking glass than your ex, there's usually some long-lasting pain or hurt that begs to be healed.

You may be wondering how that's considered villainous, but the grand double standard between villains and heroes is that when heroes punish, it's justice, but when villains do it, it's revenge. In the end, they're the same thing. Heroes wrap themselves in a delusional cloak of goodness, simply because they refuse to see themselves as villains. While heroes would like you to believe that they're greater than a villain, they aren't.

Punishing is such a basic human feeling and

motivation that we build intricate systems of governance whose sole occupation is punishing those who society deem deserving, but heroes are the ones who rule that system. Thus, only what they choose to see as wrong is worthy of punishment.

Heroes often do things as wicked as those they call villains. Whatever they do in the name of heroism is okay— whether stealing from a villain or killing a witch—and to hold them responsible for such vile actions is villainous. Heroes are the sheriffs, and villains are the vigilantes. Heroes often crave justice for others and mercy for themselves. But that's enough playing in the sandbox of morality. Back to the point.

The Punisher walks a fine line between success and failure, generally because most Punishers don't have an end goal. If you are looking to be avenged, you must decide what the price or penalty will be, exact it, and walk away. The moment it is over, you have to let it go. If you step past that, the hero will inevitably show up and beat you to a pulp.

In addition, when deciding the punishment, it's best to divorce your emotions and look at it rationally. The punishment exacted must be equal to the crime. For example, death is a completely inappropriate punishment for hurt feelings or rude behavior. Do not take a page from the hero's book and deal out death for every infraction of the law. Being passionate and having drive are musts in villainy, but allowing your heart to override logic always ends in catastrophe.

Generally, I don't work with Punishers. They tend to be

too unstable and cross lines I'm not comfortable with. Murder isn't a place I'm willing to go, nor is it necessary. There are far worse ways to punish than death, and crowing over the corpse of your fallen enemy isn't as satisfying as you think. Just remember, almost any villainous plan can be achieved without resorting to it.

I have a friend by the name Gabrielle. She's an average, ordinary fairy, with moderate talent and a rather high strung disposition. Understandably, she was hurt when she was cordially uninvited to the christening of her kingdom's princess. The king and queen claim it was a mistake, but really, they wanted to make sure the fairy blessings their little bundle of joy received were only the best of the best.

They didn't view Gabrielle's practical gifts, like the gift of sound financial investment or diplomacy, equal to the fairy standards that revolve around music, grace, and beauty. Personally, I think Gabrielle's a more fitting gift for the future ruler of a country, especially when princesses are automatically viewed as beautiful and graceful, whether true or not. Blessing a princess with that seems like a wasted magical gift.

But I digress.

Gabrielle spent months planning the perfect gift for the little princess. I don't know why she would bother blessing a baby already so fully blessed at birth, but that's the kind of person she is. Sweet, naive Gabrielle didn't recognize the obvious slight for what it was and went to the party anyway.

The greedy king and queen invited seven other fairies from various neighboring kingdoms, lavishing them with personalized gifts and attention, hoping for only the best of fairy gifts for their daughter, all while pointedly ignoring Gabrielle. Over the course of the evening, it became clear to Gabrielle just how thoroughly unwanted she was, and by the time it came to give the gifts, Gabrielle decided enough was enough. They needed to be punished.

Gabrielle cursed the princess that she would prick her finger on the spindle of a spinning wheel and die. That may seem like the exact type of overreaction I was preaching against moments ago, but Gabrielle wasn't a fool. The curse wouldn't take place for years, and she knew such curses were always easily undone in some spectacular fashion that ended with the princess happily ever aftered with some princeling. The curse caused the king and queen an equal amount of emotional turmoil they'd caused her. In fact, the curse was tweaked within minutes of its casting, and the princess recently fell into a deep sleep that will be broken by a kiss from a prince in no time.

After the party, Gabrielle packed up and left the kingdom to find a place that appreciated her skills. In the end, she realized handing out curses tended to bring more good than the gifts: it's the "evil" fairies that lead the princesses to find their happily ever after, not the good. She made a profound career shift and now specializes in curses.

Gabrielle succeeded because she had a clear goal, achieved it, and walked away. The Punisher villain fails when they hang around or are unable to see the proper stopping point. Those villains slide from punishing into sadism, eventually stirring up the hero circuit to action. If you strike, strike well, and walk away, you will achieve your goal and live a long and happy life afterwards.

Most villains slip into the role of Punisher at some point in their career. As I said, villains are a passionate lot and tend to be more sensitive than they care to let on, and those hurt feelings lead to a desire for retribution. I'm sorry if that offends anyone reading this book, but that only proves my point. Beware becoming a passing Punisher. Punishing is not a good side project. If you want this path, choose it independent of any other villainous goals you have and walk away the minute your plans are completed. Feel free to then follow other villainous paths, but trying to walk two at the same time will only lead to failure.

The Entrepreneur

As the name implies, this is the tradesman villain. They want to better their materialistic standing in the world. This is most commonly done with money, but strangely enough, babies are a close second. And don't turn your nose up at babies or other odd commodities. Bartering is still alive and well in our society, and it's amazing what you can get for a small child, talking horse, or even someone's name. Whatever the commodity, gaining that object is at the heart of their villainy.

This is a motivation near and dear to my heart. Of course, that is because I am an Entrepreneur. Besides my own emotional investment, I find this to be one of the most unjust villain categorizations. Everyone should aspire to bettering oneself, and I'm not talking in a greedy sense. If you have the ambition to work hard and try something new, you shouldn't be labeled a villain. It is a noble and good thing to build a comfortable life for yourself.

Entrepreneurs need to have a greater wit about them than other villains. Don't get me wrong, all villains need a sturdy head on their shoulders or they will lose it quicker than a princess can kiss a frog, but at the heart of this villainous path is the trade. The Entrepreneur loves to trade, and non-villains love to wiggle out of it. If you're not careful, you'll make a trade with a hero and find yourself thrown from a tower, torn in two, or chucked into a barrel full of glass, nails, and other sharp, pointy objects (all real villain deaths, I assure you). More often than not, villains are cheated by the heroes, but if you're quick on your feet, you'll make it out alive, with your prize intact.

A client of mine did this brilliantly and was able to misstep the righteous liars and cheaters to get his payment. Wilhelm dreamed of having a nice cottage and piece of land on which to raise a family. He'd worked that land his entire life, but like most farmers, his family were subject to the whims of the lord of the manor.

When this lord decided he wanted better hunting grounds, he evicted Wilhelm's family and planted their fields with trees. It didn't matter that they'd worked the land for generations or that there were no other farms to rent. Unable to buy property (another unfair facet of the peasant's life), Wilhelm took odd jobs to make ends meet. Until we met.

By connecting him with one of my fairy contractors, I procured him a special flute that allowed him to bespell any living creature. He used it to earn a fortune in the rat catching game. That may seem like a strange course of action, but it showed insightfulness. Sure, he could have used it to force the wealthy to give him a fortune or to get his revenge on the rat who stole his home, but then this story would have ended far sadder for Wilhelm. Grand schemes are fine and well, but they attract a lot of backlash.

Using his flute, he was able to lead every single rat out of a castle or town with little effort, leaving it vermin free. He didn't even bother to gouge his clients. He offered competitive rates, which added up into an incredible sum when you consider he was catching hundreds and thousands of rats in one fell swoop. Once the town was cleared and the vermin exterminated, he moved on to the next.

He went along like this for a couple years, slowly amassing the nest egg he needed, until one day he hit a snag. Where most were happy to hand over the small fortunes Wilhelm charged to clear their cities, he came across a silly hamlet that thought nothing of cheating a hardworking man from his fairly earned wages.

After Wilhelm did his job, the mayor refused to pay him a single farthing for his troubles, even threatening to arrest Wilhelm on charges of fraud, claiming he had planted trained rats. I have no doubt Wilhelm wouldn't have survived the trial if he'd been caught; in instances like that, townsfolk have a shocking tendency to form vengeful mobs, which never ends well for villains. But Wilhelm didn't get angry; he simply collected payment a different way.

Turning his flute on the children of the town, he led

them out of their beds and far away from the hamlet. Wilhelm held them until the town paid the money, plus a little extra for his troubles. Of course, the town has spread the story far and wide that he stole them or even drowned the poor kids. I even heard it said once that he sold their souls to the devil. Ludicrous. But it kept Wilhelm from ever finding another job. The minute he'd approach any town, they greeted him with torches and pitchforks. Luckily, he'd already saved enough that he could retire.

Wilhelm got the money he needed, never got cheated, and saved his own skin at the same time. So, definitely a successful endeavor. A peasant who had nothing was able to turn a generally pathetic career into a serious money maker through intelligence and prudence.

The Havocker

There are a significant portion of villains who simply like to spread a little chaos. They pop into someone's life or kingdom, curse them or take something from them or cause any other type of mayhem. The Havockers are the villains who simply want to wreak a bit of havoc.

Before my villainy consulting company focused their talents, most Havockers simply did it for the thrill of upsetting the balance, which is beyond pointless; such destruction serves no purpose. Some Havockers argue that senseless destruction can serve a purpose, but generally, they're wasting their time and talents.

Working with Havockers, I've been able to shift their focus and help them perfect their craft. Now, most

Havockers tend more towards evil-for-hire; they cause a little havoc and also get paid, while providing a valuable service. Most heroic grand adventures begin with an evil upset. Princes get turned into frogs or beasts or bears by some random enchantress and go on to find their future wife and fame while breaking the curse. It's the curses brought on by Havockers that end up acting as the catalyst for change for heroes and their heroines. Where before they provided that catalyst for free, now they are able to make a living off producing evil curses and enchantments for a fee.

Parents love hiring villains to intercede in their beloved child's lives to guarantee their kid's inclusion into the hero or heroine society. They won't dirty their lily-white hands with villainy but feel no compunction in paying someone else to do so, and villains are easier to hire than fairy godmothers. Not that it's impossible. Fairy godmothers are as corruptible as the rest of the hero set, but since they view themselves as being above bribery, it takes a lot of diplomacy and skill to haggle with them.

Now, that might sound like the contracted Havockers are falling into the Entrepreneur role, and there's some truth to that. Once money factors into the equation, the line between Havockers and Entrepreneurs gets thin. However, the difference is that with or without money exchanging hands, Havockers would be cursing people. They just finally understand how to get more than a sense of glee out of it.

Successful Havockers have a simple, two-step process—curse and leave. That's it. Do what you want and get out. If you're not around, you can't receive any retribution. It's as simple as that. Since you're only interested in causing the initial trouble, it shouldn't be difficult to walk away.

And don't fool yourself into thinking that if you're a contracted Havocker that this rule doesn't apply to you. Just because you are a hired worker doesn't mean that the people who hired you won't turn on you the minute it's in their best interest. The moment a deal is struck, a Havocker becomes an Entrepreneur, and even though you're paid for your services, your clients view you as "evil" and will try to stop you.

So Havockers, take your money and get out of the area.

The only other caution is that you need to be careful about what type of curse you place on your victims. Arming your heroes with fangs, claws, speed, and strength is not the smartest thing you can do. If you can get far away from them immediately, you'll be fine, but frogs are a much better option. You don't want to anger someone, make them more lethal, and sit waiting to see what will happen next, like a Havocker I knew by the name of Reed.

He changed a princeling into a wolf, thinking it would be much more entertaining to watch the prince/wolf scare any of the heroines who tried to break the curse. However, transformations can have adverse reactions. You're changing their entire physiology, so it's bound to have occasional side effects.

In this case, Reed wasn't the greatest of spell casters, and not only did he make the prince deadlier but rather unstable, too. The prince went on a rampage, killing Reed and then a young girl and her grandmother before he was put down by a woodsman.

Steer clear of predators. It's not a good idea.

Havocker is the simplest of villains to be. It doesn't take a ton of knowledge; some skill with magic is ideal but not necessary. There is more than one way to cause trouble, so don't limit yourself. And where subtlety or patience or self-control are required for the other types of villains, they aren't for the Havocker. Like I said, it's simply a cause-trouble-and-go job. There's not a lot to screw up, unless you pull a Reed.

Chapter Two

Setting Your Sights on the Prize

Villains are active sorts, ready to take their lives and career into their own hands and stop letting a select group of people determine what they're capable of. That is a good thing, but that drive can push them to skip important preparatory steps vital to success.

Before you even think of taking on a villainous lifestyle, you must prepare yourself, inside and out. Becoming a villain isn't as easy as buying black leather outfits and cackling maniacally.

Let me rephrase that.

Becoming a quality villain is more than buying black leather and cackling.

Being a villain is easy. Being a successful villain takes time, energy, and intelligence. Hopefully, you have those three things in spades because your success depends on them. With proper goals and plans, you can weather the uncertain variabilities that come with life to find the success you desire. Success and survival depend on planning.

Every Journey Requires a Destination

Whether taking over a kingdom or putting your uppity stepdaughter in her place, you need to have a clearly defined goal. There are the nebulous goals and motivations I outlined in the previous chapter, such as power, material gain, punishment, etc., but you need to decide the specifics of what you wish to achieve. For some, this may be difficult when you have a long-term goal without a clear end point, such as ruling a kingdom, but there are still some important questions you must ask yourself:

- Why do I want to do this?
- How far am I willing to go?

Those answers need to be in harmony with each other; otherwise, you will fail. I cannot tell you how many of my clients have been defeated because they forgot to focus on these core things. All my potential clients must have satisfactory answers to these two questions before I'll even consider taking them on.

Why do I want to do this?

Beyond the basic motivation inherent in each type of villain, there is an underlying why beneath that. Why do you want that power? Why do you want that justice? Why do you want to turn that prince into a frog? Why are you going villain rather than sticking with the life you were given? The life of a villain is not an easy one, and you need a clear understanding of your personal motivations. If you lose sight of the why, it will be infinitely harder to push through the hailstorm of crap that will come your way.

You must be clear in your motivations and not let other desires or distractions pull you from your original goal. Doing so only ends in death.

I knew a couple Entrepreneur villains who got swept up in this mistake. They weren't clients of mine, but I had encounters with them during my career, and they're some of the only partner villains I ever came across. It's not unheard of for villains to work together from time to time, but Andrew and Catherine developed a symbiotic relationship.

Catherine started in the ranks of the good fairies but grew to see the benefits of charging for her services. Powerful and talented, Catherine drew a myriad of petitioners seeking to buy her blessings. Unfortunately, many of them were people who didn't understand what "by appointment only" meant, while others refused to take her rejection seriously and showed up on her doorstep repeatedly to demand her help.

Now, Andrew was a man of little repute. Not inherently magical, he struggled to find his Entrepreneurial niche. He'd known Catherine for many years, and when she complained to him about the non-stop interruptions, he came up with a mutually beneficial plan.

Catherine placed enchanted lions at the gate of her home to protect her from uninvited guests. As many royals are too bullheaded to simply turn tail and run, she needed to have a contingency plan. She only wanted them off her doorstep, not wiped off the face of the planet.

Andrew proposed she install a trapdoor hidden in a magic orange tree to serve as an escape route, which he guarded. When an interloper got too near, Andrew emerged from it and took them to safety.

Besides giving Andrew a comfortable home inside the orange tree, Andrew was able to turn it into a lucrative opportunity. Though he had every intention of keeping the lions from eating anyone too stupid to take the hint, he used it as an opportunity to bilk the terrified twits.

Catherine got her peace and quiet, Andrew made a decent living, and royals learned to not go where they weren't wanted. Though a little complicated, the plan served their goals well.

Each lived a successful villainous life. In fact, Andrew spread the rumor that cakes pacified the lions, so not only did he have a steady income but a steady delivery of cake, too. Until Catherine and Andrew lost sight of why they were villains.

One afternoon, Andrew found a queen wandering towards Catherine's home with a basket of tell-tale cake. For some reason, she thought it a good time to take a nap, giving Andrew time to sneak away with her cakes and polish off every last crumb.

When the queen awoke, finding her cake missing and the lions bearing down on her, she panicked. Andrew appeared, demanding payment in exchange for a safe escape from the lion's jaws, and the queen immediately offered up her daughter's hand in marriage.

You see, the queen had a daughter by the name of Marie who caused her mother no end of headaches. The girl refused to marry any of the numerous suitors vying for her hand. The queen was looking for Catherine to find a way to coerce her spoiled, selfish, vain daughter into accepting one of them. At least, that's how the queen described her daughter.

Really, it wasn't Marie's shortcomings that kept her from accepting a marriage proposal—it was her suitors'. She was one of the only princesses I've heard of who wanted to marry someone she loved and respected, neither of which she found among the obtuse men she'd met.

But that's beside the point. While the queen preferred marrying her to someone "better" than Andrew, at that moment, she was only thinking of saving her own skin. It's shocking how parents willingly offer up their children as payment for some deal with a villain, but it is what it is.

Normally, Andrew would have bartered the queen down to a more reasonable payment, but he'd grown lonely over the years and longed for a family of his own. Since the only woman he lived near was his business partner who had no romantic interest in him, he looked at the situation and thought, "Why not?"

Frankly, I can think of a big reason why. Several, in fact, the most prominent of which is that he was a villain working towards the goal of financial security. If he wanted to change gears and look for love, he should have quit his job and moved into a non-villainous life. Romance and villains don't mix.

But I'm getting ahead of myself.

Andrew took the queen up on her offer, and they set a wedding date. When the queen got safely home, she instantly regretted it. After all, marrying Marie off to a villain wouldn't be politically or socially helpful in any way.

In addition, Marie didn't want to marry a stranger; the only thing she knew of him was that he lived in an orange tree and extorted people, which wasn't the most auspicious beginning to a relationship. Marie snuck away and sought out Andrew to see if he would accept another form of payment.

After meeting each other, they fell in love and decided to go ahead with the wedding. While Marie was gone, the queen colluded with one of Marie's suitors, and they decided to force the girl to marry him before her wedding to Andrew. When Marie returned, the queen and Marie's chosen fiancé forced her to the altar. Andrew found out at the last moment and enlisted Catherine's help to swoop in and rescue his fair maiden.

Stealing her away from the wedding, Andrew took Marie to safety, far from her mother and her fake fiancé. Meanwhile, Catherine was angry on Andrew's behalf and took the queen and the fake fiancé with her, determined to give them a stint in her prison to make them pay for their deceit.

I wish I had more information about what happened after this, but from here on out the story gets muddled. The victors made sure of it.

Andrew and Marie married and built a life together. They were quite happy until the fake fiancé seduced one of Catherine's maids, tricking her into helping him escape. He didn't bother releasing the queen, but killed Catherine in her sleep and went hunting for his "stolen" bride.

There are grand tales of the adventures he went on while searching for Marie, but all that matters is that when he caught up to Andrew, he was not kind. Andrew was no fighter or magician and stood no chance against a sword.

The man killed Andrew and carried Marie off, but she died before he married her. I don't know if I believe in death by broken heart, but that's the only explanation I've found for her demise. Of course, people also like to think her heart broke over the ex-suitor and not her husband.

Whether or not you agree with Andrew and Catherine's choices, the fact is that they allowed themselves to get distracted from being the Entrepreneurs they were. However righteous Catherine's anger on her friend's behalf, slipping into the Punisher role got her killed. No matter how romantic and wonderful it may sound to find the love of your life, Andrew lost focus from his villainous role to be a hero. It didn't end well for them and neither will it for you.

The same can be said if your motivations have to do with admiration or adoration. You are a villain. Period. End of discussion. Regardless of how well you treat the people or what evil you may or may not do, public opinion will automatically be against you. Following this guide will help mitigate it, but no matter what you do the general public will view you as a usurper or pot-stirrer.

Seeking gratification from others is a surefire path to destruction. If your goals hinge on a person or people giving you a specific emotional response, give up now. You may be able to subjugate and dominate, but you can't force those beneath you to love you. You may punish that hero for the offense committed, but you will never get them to admit they wronged you.

In general, people love that status quo and your actions to upset that will forever label you as a villain. If you go into this thinking that the huddled masses will thank you for it, you need to abandon your plans now and adopt a puppy instead. Even the Overlords may achieve glory, but adoration is a whole other thing. Yes, there are the exceptions. There are villains so good they do make people forget they're a villain, but those are few and far between.

If you are looking to be the fairest or richest or any other -est in the land, you may be headed in the right direction, but it is near impossible to hold onto the number one spot. Besides the fact that most of those -ests are subjective, there's always someone who can knock you out of your position. All things can be fleeting, and that needs to be acknowledged when you are making any plans for the future.

Make sure you're committed to this path because you want to achieve a concrete goal. If you want to rule the land because the inbred royal leading it doesn't have two brain cells to rub together and is slowly bleeding your land dry of money and resources, great. If you want to sit on a grand throne and watch the people of your land drop to their knees due to the overwhelming power of your awesomeness, not so great. If you want to steal that baby because there's some gaping hole in your heart, definitely not good.

There's got to be some easier way to get what you want that doesn't include the possibility of you being burned at the stake.

How far am I willing to go?

Goals are great, but if they require you to do things with which you're uncomfortable, you've got a problem. There is a direct correlation between the amount of power you attain and the effort it takes to get it. The bigger your goal, the more effort you will need to exert and the greater chance you will have to cross some moralistic line in the sand. Find your personal line and set your goals within it, but be prepared to go right up to that line.

What are you willing to do to get your goal? What are you willing to sacrifice? You may have to give up everything you love in order to obtain it. These questions need to be answered before you undertake any villainous endeavors because if you are not willing to do what it takes, you might as well stick with what you have at the moment than waste your time, effort, and life pursuing that which you are not willing to fight for.

If you want to be the Lord and High Master of some realm, you have to remember that you are going to have to pry the title from the previous owner's hands. That may include doing so to his entire family—his wife, children, and even his adorable puppy, Mr. Snuggles. If you cannot do that, settle for a smaller goal. Nothing is worse than realizing you have spent years of your life and huge stacks of money to secure yourself a kingdom only to be undone by a pair of watery brown eyes staring up at you.

Another way to ask this question is, "How evil do I want to be?"

Total commitment is essential to success. However, what you're committing to can vary from goal to goal and villain to villain. A Punisher-type evil stepmother may be focused on her stepdaughter, which often doesn't require anything more tortuous than forcing the girl into servitude or exiling her to live with seven dwarves in the woods (which is a lot crueler than you would think: most woodland dwarves tend to smell like a mixture of rotten deer meat and moldy fungi that have passed through a diarrhetic toddler).

Here are some things to ask yourself:

- Is killing an option?
- Torture?
- Imprisonment?
- Exile?
- Are you willing to do it only to people who stand in your way?
- What about innocent bystanders who unknowingly get in your way?

Not all villains will need to deal with these things, and unless you have a goal that specifically includes killing, I don't believe violence is necessary. I've yet to find a single goal that couldn't be accomplished with stealth rather than a knife to the throat, but you need to look at your goals and see if any of these things are necessary and to what level you're willing to push it.

Your Wicked Plots

After you've decided what type of villain you want to be and what your goals are, you need to figure out the way to achieve that. Without speaking with you, it's difficult to give pointed advice when it comes to the details of your plans to achieve your goals, but I can impart some wisdom when it comes to the generalities.

Keep it Simple

The core and most absolute of rules is that you need to keep your plan simple. No doubt, you have brilliant schemes bubbling in your brain right now that involve huge scale operations and coordination, each part working together in perfect harmony like a brilliantly evil clock, but remember that even the best clock is useless if even one cog slips out of joint. The more effort and coordination needed between various groups or people, the more likely things will go wrong.

You do not need to jump through elaborate hoops to prove how devious you are. If you see a simple road to victory, take it. Simple does not mean bad. Fail or succeed, no one will care about how you got to that point, only that you did or did not. If you're an Entrepreneur and the commodity you're collecting is children, is there a simpler way of getting them than tricking people into giving up their firstborns? Perhaps the solution is putting out advertisements for unwanted children. You'd be surprised how many poverty-stricken parents are willing to dump their kids in the middle of the woods rather than find a way to feed them.

I knew an Entrepreneur by the name of Pierre who couldn't grasp this concept. Marrying into wealth is a plan as old as the institution itself, and he kept it simple in the fact that he followed that time honored tradition. Where he messed up was that the simple solution wasn't enough to satisfy his villainous goals, so he twisted it until it became a convoluted, overly complicated mess.

It is more difficult for women to marry above their station, but men have a much easier time of it. It's amazing how many kings hand out their daughter's hand in marriage as a reward. Do something heroic? Here's a princess! Do something brave? Here's a princess! Do anything that pleases the king? Here's a princess. This is especially true in kingdoms with a lot of them on their hands.

However, regardless of gender, there's always a limit to how high up the marriage ladder you can climb. Without a modest fortune at his disposal, Pierre couldn't possibly marry into the level of wealth he was aiming for. He finagled his way into a modestly lucrative marriage. Not the marriage he wanted, but a stepping stone of sorts. He thought it perfectly logical to marry some gal, add her money to his coffers, kill her, use that wealth to leverage a better bride with a bigger dowry, get her money, kill her, remarry, and so on.

This is where I passed on working with him. I wanted to steer his career in a different path, but he wouldn't deviate from his plan. To him, this was a simple, two-step process: marry and kill, repeat as necessary. But murder isn't a simple thing at all. It brings a world of trouble, especially when you're killing off young, beautiful girls. People frown on that. They have no problem leaving their kids out in the woods to die, but killing heroines is a big no-no.

Frankly, murder in general is unnecessary and only complicates plans. There are so many other ways to get what you want without resorting to brutality. Even Punishers can get their end goal without resorting to it. Leave murder to the heroes. They may have no compunction with playing judge, jury, and executioner, but I advise my clients against it.

Of course, Pierre wasn't happy with my rejection and refused to listen to the bit of free advice I gave him before he struck off on his own. He made it through a handful of brides before being killed by the last. I'm not sorry to see the world rid of a man of his ilk. The guy was a sociopath, not a true villain. I have no idea why people kept sending him girls to wed, but that's just a lesson to never underestimate the power of greed. None of us are immune.

Compare that disastrous result to a client of mine, Edward. He had a goal, came up with a plan that was simple and straightforward, achieved it, and found great success as an Overlord.

Near his home, there was a kingdom with an aging king and his only daughter. The king was of the classic royal mindset that anyone who married his daughter would need to fulfill some grand quest or challenge. He went through a list of ideas, beginning with slaying a dragon that lived in the northern most mountains. When no one completed that task, he switched gears to plucking a golden feather from a griffin. When nothing came of that, the king switched again, going for something easier, like plucking a flower that grows in some ridiculously remote and dangerous place.

It kept on like that for a few years. The king would declare a quest and either none of the princes would take it on or they'd fail spectacularly. Not that I can blame them. If I had to choose between simply kissing a dead-looking girl and facing impending death by grappling with some monster, I'd choose...actually, neither of those options sounds all that great. Princesses are never worth the hassle.

Regardless of my own feelings on the relative lack of enticements when it comes to princesses, the king kept trying to hook a son-in-law to take over the kingdom. With his health failing fast, he grew more and more desperate. If his wife had been alive, she would have simply hired a curse for her daughter to draw in a prince, but the king was stuck with the idea that his daughter's husband needed to prove himself.

Granted, I think his logic was far more sound than that of a cursing. At least with a quest, you get someone who has ability. Most cursed princesses end up with the guy who puckers up first. And kissing a curse away isn't an ability. It doesn't even need to be a good kiss to break a curse.

But I've gotten sidetracked. Royals are such a bizarre and confusing bunch, we can drive ourselves crazy trying to understand their logic.

In a final attempt to get a successor, the king declared a new quest. Anyone who made his daughter laugh would get her hand in marriage and inherit the kingdom. This seemingly easy quest attracted heroes by the droves. Unfortunately, this particular princess was of a dour temperament. Princesses tend to use giggling as their primary mode of communication, but this princess was of an unusual temperament.

I would have to say that this is one of the best quests I've ever heard of. Not because of its ease, but because of its significance. The king wanted someone proven to make his daughter happy. I hate to admit that any crazy royal scheme has merit, but I would say that the king had the right idea, though whether or not it was intentional is up for debate.

Enter Edward. He heard about this and wanted to take a stab at it, but not being a prince meant he had no chance to try. That is the only part of the king's scheme that was ridiculous—the king still insisted that non-royals need not apply. A gross oversight. And one I was definitely willing to work around.

Edward needed something of epically silly proportions and visible from a distance. Anyone outside of royalty who showed up to try their luck was turned away, unable to meet the girl, but the princess was known to watch the city from a particular window, so we didn't need to get the king involved if she could see it from the window.

Looking at the previous princely attempts, we determined the things that hadn't worked, and it left us with a very narrow window (pun not intended). The closest thing to a laugh any of the princes had gotten was a snort, and that was because he'd tripped over his own feet and fell into a punch bowl. But princes won't intentionally make idiots of themselves, so none of the others had been brave enough to take the tom-foolery route. They'll face man-eating trolls and fire-breathing dragons, but pretend to fall on their face? No way.

So we knew what route to take, but most physical comedy isn't impactful at a distance. Enlisting a contractor, we had a magic goose commissioned. The sorcerer made the goose golden in appearance to entice people to touch it. However, once touched, the magic held onto the toucher, forcing them to remain stuck to the bird. To add to the impact, the magic extended to anyone affixed to the bird, making them as sticky as the goose. Armed with his magic, Edward walked into the center of town.

Within moments, someone tried to steal a feather from the goose, which made them stick. When others tried to pry that person free, they joined the motley crew, growing and stringing out until dozens of people and animals were squirming and shrieking, trying to get free. Normally, I have too many things going on to watch over each client during every step of their plans, but this was one that I couldn't miss. I can't describe how funny it was to see Edward parading this mass of people around.

Far above us, the princess watched, unable to stop laughing.

I was worried for a moment that the king wouldn't honor his decree, but the king kept his word. Most likely, he was desperate to get the succession firmly situated.

Edward achieved everything he wanted by simply making someone laugh. The fact is that most kings and queens have several children—if not dozens, in some cases—and they don't have the resources to give them all land of their own. A kingdom wouldn't last long if they divided it equally between their kids and the grandchildren, and so on.

Where lower class families want kids for a built-in workforce (unless work is slow, in which case the kids are "downsized" by tossing them into the woods), royals have no need for multiple children, except as an heir, a spare, and to attract marriage alliances with other kingdoms. A king and queen's best option is to marry them off to other kingdoms, but there's not always enough royal alliances to go around. Sometimes they get desperate and become willing to elevate anyone who will take their excess princes and princesses off their hands.

So don't overcomplicate it. Sometimes the simplest of plans yield great rewards.

Before I move onto the next section, I would like to take a moment to discuss coercion. Manipulating people is extremely fun. There is a wonderful sense of power that comes from getting people to dance to your tune without them knowing it, but coercion is nothing more than manipulation's inbred cousin.

There are arguments to be made for the benefit of using coercion at times, but in most instances, it simply complicates things. Once coercion is used, your plans become reliant on unwilling participants.

More often than not, coerced people suffer some great pains of conscience and back out, leaving you in the lurch and most likely tied to a pyre. Or they'll fight you every step of the way once the initial fear that pushed them to agree is gone. Think back to Andrew extorting the queen before he'd save her from the lions; the queen was willing at first (she was the one who suggested Andrew marry her daughter in the first place), but once the looming threat was gone, the queen became Andrew's greatest opposition to him marry her daughter.

Don't trust that blackmail or a previous agreement will be enough for them to change their moral compass. People are more than willing to put aside their morality if it brings some benefit to them, but doing so unwillingly tends to make people cling to those morals tighter than they would otherwise. People resent being forced to do things, even if they'd normally do it of their own free will.

If you need people on your side and they're not willingly helping you, they're more likely to mess things up or turn on you. If your plans rely on it, go back to the drawing board. I guarantee there's a simpler way to do it.

Plan B

Flexibility isn't only for acrobats. Though you may have the perfect plan, you need to accept that life is life, and not everything works out perfectly. Sometimes there are issues. Sometimes the hero shows up at the absolute wrong time. Sometimes the kindly parents who promised you their firstborn child back out. You never know what will happen, so you must be prepared for the unexpected.

A backup plan is an absolute necessity. You need to figure out what other options are available to get your end goals and what you're willing to settle for because even the best laid plans aren't guaranteed to be successful.

As the saying goes, there's more than one way to curse a prince, and you need to keep that in mind. There are other avenues that can get you the same outcome, so decide the best one to take and then have the second best ready just in case.

However, changing to Plan B should only be done after serious consideration, and if you choose to move to it, don't go back to Plan A. Never go back to a plan after it has failed. Let it go.

And even if you have the most perfect Plan A and Plan B (or even C, D, E, and F), not everyone gets what they want in the end. Even with perfect planning, there may be unforeseeable hiccups, and you need to decide what you'll settle for. If you want world domination, would you be happy with only a kingdom? Would simply surviving be enough?

Too many villains believe in the "success or bust" mentality. They view anything else as absolute failure and not worth contemplating. But it's not. Not all plans work out and that's okay, but if you refuse to acknowledge that sometimes the best plan is an escape, you're cutting off the opportunity to regroup and come back swinging.

Escape plans aren't cowardly. They're smart. If you see your plans crumbling and the hero charging at you, I know you will not be thinking in that moment that death is better than failure. Surviving is not weakness. Retreating is strategic and necessary at times, and you need to plan for it now. Just in case.

Focus

When executing your schemes, you must keep your eye

on the prize. While flexibility is important, you should only change tactics when necessary and not do so lightly. Every time you course correct, you risk losing time and resources, not to mention your focus. Keep your goals in the forefront of every plan you make.

The villainy types are not set in stone, but you should not switch types willy-nilly. It must further your end goal (such as using the Entrepreneur role in order to finance your larger villainy plans as a Counselor or Overlord) or be a complete career shift.

I shared Gabrielle's story earlier, and she's a perfect example of how to successfully shift between villain types. Gabrielle began as a Punisher, seeking to punish the king and queen who were so callously rude to her at their daughter's christening. Once she achieved that, she moved into a Havocker villain because she enjoyed the good that a little chaos produces. When I met her and discussed the entrepreneurial opportunities out there, she moved into an Entrepreneur role. Each time, she had a goal she wanted to achieve and when she either A) achieved it or B) discarded it, she moved on.

Never, ever try to sit in two roles at the same time. Many of my clients struggle to remember this, especially since many villains veer off into Punisher mode. Life takes a turn and you want to punish the person responsible. Makes sense. However, when that punishment takes you away from your main focus, it's a problem.

Letting things like your pride or vengeance or small squabbles take your focus away from what you are trying to accomplish will only land you in trouble. Almost every single one of my clients' failures can be tied to this principle. They allow themselves to get caught up in petty issues that don't further their cause. Petty issues make for petty criminals.

I worked with a client by the name of Suzanne, who wanted to be an Overlord. Through splendid planning and effort on our part, she became queen of a kingdom. Her husband was so uninterested in his job that he left the ruling entirely to Suzanne. It was a perfect situation. But just because you accomplished what you set out to do, it doesn't mean it can't all go away. For those of you who are Overlords and Counselors, remember that yours is a long-standing goal. Even if you feel like you've achieved it, it's not over until you retire.

People who use the villain's path to gain what they want can lose it at any moment. Where heroes and heroines reach a point where they get all they wanted and can live happily ever after, you, my dear villain, won't reach that point. Your life won't be hanging in the balance at every moment, but if you attract the ire of a hero, you'll be in trouble regardless of how successful you've been up to that point.

Getting back to my original point, Suzanne forgot this. She had gained the life she wanted and thought all was good. I even felt like things would be fine, except she had the troubling habit of being fixated on her appearance. Now, I can't completely fault her for it. Non-villains tend to categorize attractive people as "good" and ugly as "bad", so if your beauty slips down the attractiveness scale, it can be cause for concern. Not to mention that it was her face that made her climb to power possible.

However, this fixation slipped into obsession when she commissioned a special mirror to tell her how her beauty ranked among the women in the land. Life was good until the day the mirror announced that Suzanne's stepdaughter had grown fairer than she. A pretty face can cause problems. A few flutters of eyelashes and a flirtatious smile can start wars. In Suzanne's case, she gained her position by being the most beautiful woman in the land, which caught the eye of the king. Now her stepdaughter usurped that position and had a troubling amount of enmity towards her stepmother. But that could have been dealt with. Easily.

The bigger problem was Suzanne's own insecurities that drove her to hate the girl more and more every day. Rather than orchestrating some plan that would marry the girl off and get her out of the kingdom, Suzanne grew more obsessed with getting rid of her permanently.

Against my wishes, she decided to kill the girl. Again, there are so many other ways to get rid of troublesome stepchildren that don't involve death or cursing them. That was her first mistake. The second was having her huntsman do it. It took only two bats of the girl's eyes for the guy to crumble and turn against Suzanne. He saved the stepdaughter, and the girl escaped into the woods.

Suzanne thought life was good until she checked her mirror and found the girl shacked up with a group of dwarves in the woods. This is the third and biggest mistake Suzanne made. The girl was gone, out of her hair, and unable to mess with Suzanne's plans. She'd eventually find some prince, marry, and go off to his kingdom and leave Suzanne in peace, but Suzanne's anger grew out of control until it wasn't enough to simply banish her. Suzanne needed her wiped off the face of the planet.

Not once but twice, Suzanne failed to poison the girl, but she wouldn't give up. On the third time, the poison finally took, but of course, the girl wasn't dead. Not really. Just cursed to look dead, and the next prince who wandered by woke her up. Why a guy would want to kiss a corpse, I don't know, but that's between him and his therapist.

In most instances, heroes and heroines won't bother dealing with villains if they're no longer in the picture. Once happily ever aftered, they ride off into the sunset and generally forget about the villain who brought them together. But being that aggressive made certain the prince and her stepdaughter only felt safe if Suzanne was dead. They tricked Suzanne into attending their wedding, ambushed her, strapped red-hot iron shoes to her feet, and forced her to dance for their entertainment until she died.

And they call villains evil.

Suzanne had been happy with the Overlord role, but she let her focus shift and split when she became obsessed with Punishing her stepdaughter. It could be argued that at first, it began with a desire to keep her Overlord status, but it devolved into an obsession that drew her to Punishing.

Any one of the villain types are difficult to maintain and achieve success in, but trying to tackle two at the same time is ludicrous. Always remember that heroes and pitchfork-wielding townsfolk are two steps behind you, and if you misstep, they will get you. The only successful villains are the ones who keep their focus on what's important.

Chapter Three

Taking a Look Within

Getting your plans in order is important but getting you in order is even more so. You must take stock of who you are. That might sound irritatingly psychological and unnecessary, but you are your worst enemy. You may be saying to yourself that Prince Not-So-Charming is the real threat, but more villains end up thwarted because they let their issues get in the way. It is horrifying to run the marathon and trip on the finish line—especially if at the finish line you are crowned king of all you survey. And the metaphorical trip lands you in an execution. Villains aren't generally defeated by armies. They're defeated by a single person. Don't let that defeat come from within.

Most villains skip over this step or put more focus on

the physical preparation than the emotional, and that's a huge mistake. As much as you may want to, don't skip this section. You may think you're fine, but I haven't worked with a single villain who hasn't needed some of the help offered here.

Yes, you are a villain. And yes, you probably have unresolved issues like most people—villains, heroes, and non-villains alike. However, that doesn't mean you should leave them unresolved. You are a villain, not a bundle of neurosis. If you have daddy or mommy issues, paranoias, phobias, or any number of problems, they need to be addressed or you are setting yourself up for failure.

Think of yourself like a fortress. You have big, strong walls built up to protect your plans and guard your secrets, but each of those little "quirks" in your personality is like a secret passageway. They may be left undisturbed for most of your villainous career, but at the worst possible moment, the hero will use it to his advantage. It does no good to be a Dark Lord, High and Mighty of All He Surveys if you crumble at the sight of a long-lost family member.

There is no shame in fixing your problems, but there is shame in failing spectacularly because of a fixable issue. Until you are able to embrace those parts of your personality, make sure to keep those weak points under wraps. Old crones and hermits are good at ferreting out weaknesses and love sharing it with any puppy-eyed hero or heroine that gives her a smile.

Morality and Conscience

Morals and scruples are fluid things. Though heroes will

try to convince you otherwise, they are not fixed points. There are areas of life that are black and white, but most sit comfortably in the gray. You need to figure out what lines you will or will not cross and keep firm against the morality others may impose on you. People in your life will try to convince you that you are doing wrong, but as long as you have your moral compass, you need not let the ideas of others alter your course.

For example, natural born kings feel they have a moral right to rule because it's their birthright, but a villain believes they have the moral right to rule because of their capability. They both believe they have the moral high ground, but which is right?

I am not going to outline my own morality rules, but I will advise you to figure out your own and stick to it. If you feel your action is justified, don't let someone come along and convince you that you behaved badly. You are a villain and you need to accept that you will be doing things others view as reprehensible. If their opinion matters to you, you are in the wrong profession. It is better to understand and accept that now than to come to the realization that you feel bad about what you're doing just as you're about to cross the finish line.

In a kingdom not far from here, there was a miller with more ego than sense. He made up a whopper of a story, claiming his daughter spun straw into gold. There are so many things wrong with his thought process, but I don't claim the man had any brains in his head. Word of the boast reached the king, who used that bad combination of ennui and entitlement otherwise known as royal prerogative to call the man out on it. The king took the girl, locked her in a room with a bunch of straw and told them if she did it, he would marry her. If not, he'd execute her.

Let me stop for a moment to point out the relative morality of royals. They never use the word kill—always execute. Execute implies a deserved punishment not murder. Even if the girl had nothing to do with her idiot father's actions or words, in the minds of the masses she deserves her punishment. After all, she's being executed not murdered. And now's not the time to get into the massively skewed punishment to offense ratio the royals use; in any normal situation, being caught in a lie isn't punishable by death. More on that later.

But getting back to the point of this story, a client named Tom had been waiting for a prime moment like this. Desperation often drives people to make regrettable deals, and this miller's daughter—the possible future queen—was at that point. As I've said before (and will say again), people are more than willing to give up their beloved children to save their own skin, even more so with hypothetical future children.

Tom knew this and planned to take the child, raise it, and then stage a miraculous return of the missing heir to the throne. Being the doting and loving adoptive father, he would take his place at the right hand of the throne.

All in all, a little complicated, but not a terrible way of leveraging the Entrepreneur role in order to achieve the desired Counselor role.

Swooping in, Tom helped the miller's daughter for a small fee. He knew he would not be able to get her to agree to the baby-swap right away, so he was patient. Tom understood royalty and knew the king would never stick to his word after only one night (another example of the fluidity of royal morality).

When the king saw the miller's daughter succeed—like all royal high-and-mighty, center-of-the-universe, back dealing dolts—he got greedy and said she had to do it another night. Granted, Tom did spread rumors about how she faked the whole thing, guaranteeing the king would want another test.

Tom came back the next night and helped her again, only to have the king react the same way. On the third day, the miller's daughter had nothing left to barter. Begging him for his help, she offered up anything he wanted. Without a moment's hesitation, the loving future mother gave up her child and claimed her crown the next day.

Of course, it didn't take long before the miller's daughter bore a child, and Tom came to claim the princeling. Despite the convoluted nature of his plan, things came together nicely. Until he saw the tears.

Heroines are always beautiful. Lovely, sweet, kind, and with the potent ability to cry at the drop of a hat. It's like they have a magic about them that makes people want to swoop in and save them from their own selves. Tom stood no chance; he let his moral grip slip.

He agreed to a new bargain, giving her three days to guess Tom's name. This is probably a good time to remind you that Tom isn't his real name. Besides protecting client confidentiality, swapping out his true name for something shorter is a bit of a necessity. Writing out Tom's real name is so ridiculously long that I can never spell it correctly.

In all honesty, what he chose for the clause wasn't a bad idea. On her own, the heroine would never guess his name. But he was trying to assuage his guilt and guarantee his success at the same time. He should have let go of the guilt and stuck to the cardinal rule of Entrepreneurs: take your winnings and leave.

A heroine on her own isn't generally a problem, but heroines attract problem causing heroes. In this case, the heroine already had one. The king was ignorant of his wife's bargain, but letting her delay paying the piper only invited more time and opportunities for the king to get involved.

The new queen spent the first day guessing every name that came to mind. On the second, she sent messengers far and wide to find unusual names and guessed those. By the third day, the king noticed something was wrong and confronted her. If you expected him to get angry at his wife for her lies and deceit, you'd be wrong. Another example of fluid morality, the king may have doled out death for her father's lies, but she was now his wife and mother of his heir and thus blameless. Never mind that he would have executed her if he had known of the bargain before their marriage. All blame landed on Tom's poor head.

When he showed up the final day, the king's guards captured him, and the king and queen reneged on the deal the queen had so eagerly agreed to—twice. The common rumor roaming the realms is that in a fight of arrogance, Tom was caught dancing around the woods, calling out his name, which the queen's messengers overheard and revealed to her. Tom then got so angry he ran off and was never heard of again. I even heard one person swear Tom got so mad he ripped himself in half. But which is more likely, that he had the strength to rip his body in half or the victorious heroes did it for him?

If Tom hadn't allowed his guilt to keep him from taking the child when he first showed up, he would have gotten everything he wanted. Heroes and heroines don't allow black and white morality to stop them from what they want, so why do you? I'm not saying that you need to go as dark as they go, but don't let their regrets keep you from your victory.

Insecurities versus Pride

I once read about a correlation between being insecure and prideful. Rather than being opposites of each other, they are inseparable. A person with raging insecurities often has at least one area of their life in which they are excessively arrogant and proud. The opposite is true about arrogant and proud people. It's the way they balance their personality. Pride and insecurities aren't separate entities. They go hand-in-hand.

Villains must keep this in mind. As I've said before, by your very nature, you are a confident person. You need to be. You are choosing a path that is different from the norm, and that requires you to have a solid sense of self. However, you must not mistake arrogance for confidence.

A prideful villain makes stupid decisions based on their belief that they are stronger or better than they are. It pushes villains to ignore good advice or underestimate heroes and heroines. Then their insecurity rears its head, upsetting their plans further when it drives them to seek out the approval and reassurance of others, leaving them dependent on others for their sense of self-worth.

Validation is unattainable for a villain. You are a villain and are doing things that by your very title go against what most believe to be "good", so no one is going to be lining up to shake your hand when you win. No one is cheering for you or will be waiting to compliment you, so looking to them for validation is a useless waste of time.

Someone with true self-esteem will view their abilities and talents with a realistic eye and won't fluctuate between pride and insecurity, regardless of the situation. Not to say that they won't have high or low moments, but on the whole, they remain steady. You need to find that balance. Too many villains fall prey to debilitating insecurities that make them overcompensate with heavy-handed doses of pride that pop up at the worst times.

Humility is not the anathema most villains view it to be. Pride isn't strength and humility isn't weakness. It is understanding and acknowledging that you're human and imperfect. It's not weakness to have a realistic opinion of yourself.

Near my home, there lived a mother with two daughters, both beautiful enough to qualify for heroine status. The younger had the perfect, spineless temperament fit for a future princess, but the eldest wanted to take a different route.

At that young time in my life, I didn't have the necessary villainy knowledge to understand just what Lotta was, but looking back, I realize she was a Counselor villain in the making. Lotta wanted wealth, status, and power without being tied in marriage to some prince. Instead, she leveraged her sister's prospects. Following much the same path as Charles (see "The Counselor" section of Chapter One), Lotta decided that lowering her sister's situation to elicit magical help was just what was needed.

Luckily for Lotta, her mother didn't need much prompting to make her sister's life difficult. Before long, the girl's life became unbearable with her overbearing mother forcing her to do every menial task.

One day, her sister trekked several miles to the nearby well. After drawing up some water, an old beggar woman approached her, asking for a drink. The sister gave it over without thought, and the beggar woman revealed herself to be a fairy. Being not only beautiful but also kind, the fairy blessed the younger sister that every time she opened her mouth, flowers and precious stones would fall from it.

Now, I'm not sure why being nice and pretty makes someone deserving of eternal wealth or why that wealth needs to appear in such an odd way, but that is what happened. Fairies have a sadistic sense of humor sometimes.

Lotta's younger sister returned home, showing them the gift she'd been granted, and Lotta saw a new opportunity. Lotta decided she didn't need to be dependent on her sister for future happiness. She wanted her own independent wealth.

But Lotta's pride got in the way. Not only the pride of being unwilling to live off her sister's bounty, but her arrogance at believing she understood all the rules to the magic game. Arriving at the well, she found a beautiful, finely dressed lady instead of an old beggar woman.

She didn't take a moment to think about how strange it was for such a lady to be wandering out in the forest alone. Lotta only saw someone who might ruin her chances of attracting the fairy in beggar woman disguise. Lotta brushed off the woman, angering the fairy in rich lady disguise.

Lotta got what she wanted—a fairy gift—but not in the way she hoped. Instead of flowers and precious jewels, frogs and snakes dropped from her mouth.

Pride made Lotta throw aside patience and grab at the first option she saw. Pride made Lotta believe she perfectly understood the rules to the magic world. Thinking she only needed to repeat her sister's actions, Lotta's tunnel vision kept her from seeing she was wrong. I have no idea what happened to Lotta. Soon after the gift, the younger sister married some prince and left the village, and Lotta was run out of town when the amphibian and reptile infestation ruined the crops.

Lotta was the first true villain I ever knew, and she helped me understand the importance of humility—even in a villain. Lotta's confidence pushed her to be active in her life, but her pride pushed her to blind arrogance.

There's a fine line between ego being a strength and a weakness. All villains need a healthy dose of pride, that deep-down belief you can achieve your goals. If you do not believe that, why do you want to do this in the first place? But when that pride and ego pushes you to believe you are invincible, you have already lost.

Anger

Anger shows itself in many ways and only a few of them are useful to a villain. Raging about does no good. It does not solve problems and often ends up with you dead. Villains are passionate people. That may offend some of you reading this, as if it in some way emasculates you, but it's true. The amount of work and drive needed to succeed generally comes with a heavy dose of passion. That fire pushing you to villainy may push you to lash out or make stupid decisions.

I worked with a dwarf by the name of Blaine. He hired me to help find a niche in the Havocker-for-Hire industry.

It's primarily dominated by women—fairies and enchantresses, mostly—and dwarves are not known for their magical abilities. While not a requirement to be a Havocker, to be a professional requires magical ability in order to curse wealthy princes and princesses.

Using my contacts, I acquired a set of enchanted jewels that allowed Blaine to transform someone into a bear. Now, if you remember, I mentioned in the Havocker section that transforming people into predators isn't a good idea. Unfortunately, we had limited options, but we had a solid escape plan in place that allowed him to disappear before the enchanted bear could get hold of him.

Blaine leveraged a curse contract with a king and queen whose son needed an incentive to get His Royal Laziness out of the castle. Fulfilling his end of the contract, Blaine slipped away before the prince found him. Everything seemed fine, except the curse still didn't push the prince to do much. His parents had their hearts in the right place, but getting cursed doesn't magically flip off the lazy switch. He was the same person before the curse as he was after, and it took him an inordinately long time to break it. He wandered the forest, even pleading for a set of sisters who lived in the woods to take care of him. He spent the winter living on their hard work.

Meanwhile, Blaine hung around the area. He wasn't in the immediate path of the cursed prince, but he refused to leave, wanting to make sure the curse ran its proper course. Just when I had almost convinced Blaine to move on, in walked the heroine. Or I should say heroines.

Blaine had multiple run-ins with the sisters who sheltered the cursed prince. Blaine was exceptionally accident-prone and found himself always falling into trouble in full view of the heroines. He got his beard stuck a few times and the girls cut him loose, which only made him angry. Besides the fact that it's embarrassing to need help in such a vulnerable position, to get it from a heroine is beyond the pale, and Blaine felt it keenly.

Over a period of a few weeks, a pattern emerged. Blaine would get in trouble and the girls would swoop in to save him. At the heart of his problem was insecurity and pride battling back and forth, but those could have been dealt with if they hadn't driven him to anger.

Pride pushed him to cover his insecurities with anger, and that anger festered and grew, infecting his every thought. He became fixated on the girls, convinced that it was their fault and they needed punishing.

Anger forced all logic out of his mind, and Blaine slipped into the role of Punisher. Going after the girls, he tried to make them pay, but he forgot that even the laziest of princes may be incited to action if a pretty girl (or girls) is in trouble. Blaine went after the heroines, and for the first time in his life, the bear-prince did something.

Killing Blaine, the prince broke the curse and married one of the sisters. I heard that his equally lazy brother nabbed onto that success and married the other sister, but that isn't particularly important.

Blaine was foolish. Not only prone to pride and insecurities (which I covered in the previous section), he suffered from a hot temper. This combination is deadly to villains. Pride is dangerous for many reasons, and one of them is that it feeds the fire of anger. A raging forest fire burns and kills indiscriminately; don't let yourself get caught in its path.

Chapter Four

The Ups and Downs of Stereotypes

S tereotypes for villains are alive and well for a reason and not only because non-villains insist on them. Villains often fall into thinking in terms dictated by the tales we hear. The non-villains perpetuate their beliefs about what a villain is, and villains reinforce it because they are afraid of not being recognized for what they are unless they act in the "villainous" way.

It's easy to fall into the trap of thinking you need to act and look like a "villain" to be a villain. From the lowliest peasant to the highest king, people have certain expectations when it comes to us. When you ask them, depending on gender or villain type, an instant picture will pop into their head of what they would look like. Witches are stooped, covered in warts, with hair like knotted twine. Male Overlords wear all black to hide the bloodstains of the innocents they've killed. Female villains are seductresses or hideous, child-eating monsters.

Because villains are raised with these preconceived notions, they feel invalid unless they're living up to them, but overcompensating via fashion or fortress is a sure sign of insecurities. This is one of the many reasons I love working with the Counselor; not needing that validation is part of their job description.

Please stop perpetuating this horrific cycle. What's most important is being an effective villain, not creating effect.

Non-villains can be exceptionally trusting and none too bright. If they see a dirty, old woman who lives in the woods, they'll assume witch and rid themselves of her whether it's true or not. If they see a handsome young man walking through the forest in nice armor and a swagger in his step, they'll assume he's a nobleman trolling the woods for a devastatingly beautiful peasant girl to marry.

If you understand these assumptions and dress appropriately, it will help hide what you are, making it easier to achieve your goals without the heroes rising up against you. The best defense against them is to not let them know you're there. That's why the Counselor is so successful.

A client of mine by the name of Isaac was born the third son of a middle class family. Not interested in power or domination, Isaac sought for a more comfortable life than his middle class upbringing afforded. Unfortunately, Isaac didn't have the skills to follow the Entrepreneur route. Luckily, he was self-aware enough to know that he didn't have it in him, and we searched for another avenue.

In a kingdom not far from Isaac's home, there was a very wealthy king. A very wealthy king in desperate need of a son-in-law. Unfortunately, this king's daughter was of a particularly difficult temperament. In plain terms, she wasn't pretty enough for princes to put up with her attitude. Which is saying a lot.

Having married off the rest of his kids, the king was stuck with this final daughter who annoyed any suitor who came calling. He'd even tried magical means to snare a suitable husband for her, but from the rumors I heard, all it took was a few words from her mouth to convince the guy to bolt. Short of a sleeping curse, there wasn't much her father could do. But most sleeping curses work best on infants because they need years to germinate before they're at their most potent.

So, Isaac saw an opportunity for all three parties to get what they wanted. If he convinced the king and his daughter that he was a prince long enough for the two of them to marry, he'd get a life in the lap of luxury, the princess would get a husband, and the king could stop worrying about finding her a husband.

It's easy to trick royals into thinking you're something you're not. As stated before, by acting like one of them and eschewing the normal villain stereotypes, they won't see what you are. Knowing the propensity of princes to get cursed into animal form, he hired himself a curse and turned into a lowly frog. I took him to a spring deep in the woods where the princess was known to wander, and we waited. And waited. And waited. It took a ridiculous amount of time, but our patience paid off.

For some strange reason, the princess had a golden ball

she loved to toss around. Personally, that seems like it would be too heavy and easily dented or damaged to play with, but royals aren't known for their logic.

With a little behind the scenes management, we were able to get the girl to drop it right into the deepest part of the spring. Enter the slimy, green Isaac. Within moments, he got her to agree to let him come home with her if he got the ball back. For princesses, talking animals are not an uncommon occurrence, so she didn't bat an eye at the talking frog and agreed. Of course, the princess reneged and ran off without Isaac, but we weren't so easily discouraged.

I got him to the castle, and he drew the attention of the king. While the princess brushed the frog off, the king looked at Isaac and grabbed onto the idea that Isaac must be a cursed prince. Though the king played it off like he was forcing her to keep her word, the truth was that he saw an opportunity. After all, it's unheard of for someone less exalted than a royal to catch the attention of a Havocker; cursing an accountant or baker doesn't wreak much havoc.

The king opened the castle gates and ushered Isaac inside. Following the prescribed antidote for the enchantment, Isaac spent three days with the princess, dining off her plate and even sleeping on her pillow.

Yes, it wasn't the most normal of ways to break a curse, but we both agreed it would be easier than getting the girl to kiss or fall in love with him. Whether she realizes she's breaking the curse or not, once broken, that princess is tied to the former accursed, so we thought it the best option.

The king had them married the moment Isaac transformed back without bothering to ask about Isaac's background or find out if Isaac had a kingdom for her to go to. He saw an enchanted frog and assumed it was a prince.

When the truth came out, the king couldn't even get that upset about it because Isaac never lied. Not once. He never had to say he was a prince because the king never thought a villain would come in frog's clothing.

Of course, the king did give a half-hearted attempt to dispose of his son-in-law, but it was easily bested and never repeated. The king hated having a single daughter more than having a peasant son-in-law. Since then, Isaac has been living a comfortable life with his wife and father-in-law.

The line between hero and villain is thin. Deeds alone do not always make it clear to an outsider as to who is a hero or a villain. Where many villains fall short is that they buy into the stereotypes, believing they need them in order to be an actual villain.

If you find yourself leaning towards any stereotypical villain costuming and behaviors such as full body leather, goatees, maniacal laughter, and the likes, remember that stooping to stereotypes may be fun at times, but they are distracting. And not in a good way. Let your actions speak for themselves, and leave theatrics to the theaters. Besides, no one likes an affected accent.

Going against type confuses heroes and non-villains. Bright, cheery colors are a must. Wilhelm dressed in an array of colors when working as a rat catcher (see "The Entrepreneur" section of Chapter One). No one realized they were making a deal with a villain until the bill came. No one looking at him thought him villainous, making it easier to sell his services. You don't need to go to that extreme, but do not pick out clothing that is severe. If you're not one for vibrant colors, that's fine, but steer clear of black. Even if it's what you'd normally wear, don't.

And I shouldn't have to include this, but keep yourself tidy and hygienic. Even if you are a witch, there's nothing wrong with a little soap and perfume. The key is to make yourself look unremarkable. If people don't notice you, they won't suspect you. You don't have to make yourself some fashionable fop, but most non-villains equate beauty with goodness and ugliness with evil. Either way, people don't expect an average, nondescript person to be a fountain of villainy.

Chapter Five

A Strong and Sturdy Fortress

No matter how big or small your plans, you need a solid base of operations where you can plan your grand and glorious victory. Though I use the term fortress often in this chapter, do not mistake that to mean this doesn't apply to small-scale villains as well as large-scale ones. You may not need a massive castle set in the mountains, but everyone has some form of a stronghold. Even in a smaller operation, victory may slip through your fingers if your "fortress" is poorly managed.

Design

A proper fortress begins with proper design. Unless you

are an architect, you do not have the skills or knowledge to build a sound building. Do not design it yourself. It would be like hiring a minstrel as an assassin.

You will be facing a wide variety of obstacles in your path to victory, and the one thing you do not want to worry about is whether or not your walls will withstand the armies knocking at your door or the hero breaking in. You have better things to think about—like all the things you are going to do when the huddled masses are bowing at your feet.

You may think trusting anyone else with all the secrets of your inner sanctum is ludicrous, but there should not be any secrets to begin with. Secret passages and hidden nooks are the hero's playground. No matter how jealously you guard those secrets, some crone or hermit will find out and tell any fool who crosses their path. You will be celebrating your impending victory when some trouble maker will pop out of the "secret" passage and thwart you. Massively thick walls with hulking gates do little good if you provide alternative entrances.

And before you think to solve that problem by disposing of the architect, ask yourself if you really want local contractors believing you will kill them if they work for you. It will not engender any loyalty and will make it much harder to find good help. Plus, it does no good whatsoever in keeping those forest-dwelling crones from spreading your fortress's secrets; despite countless hours spent trying to unravel that mystery, I haven't figured out how they always know.

I have a friend named Veronica. She'd worked hard during her villainy career and planned a comfortable retirement where she enjoyed the fruits of her labor. With her wicked ways behind her, she thought her life would be peaceful, but non-villains have long memories and unforgiving hearts.

Veronica came from the classic villain mentality and dressed the part. Though retired, she didn't think to steer clear of her stereotypical witch clothing. The townsfolk and her neighbors didn't break out the pitchforks and light the torches, but Veronica was surrounded by whispers and dirty looks, which isn't that big of a deal until those whispers lead to action.

Where normal villagers wouldn't think of stealing from their neighbors, they have none of the same moralistic issues when it comes to stealing from a witch. One day, Veronica caught a greedy neighbor stealing from her garden. The man's wife craved some herb or vegetable that grew in Veronica's garden. Rather than act with any modicum of decorum or sense of propriety, such as knocking on the front door and offering to buy or trade for it, the husband broke into Veronica's garden to steal some.

As if once was not bad enough, he did so again. It wasn't until the third time the guy broke in that Veronica caught him in the act and confronted him. He made his apologies and offered her anything she wanted in payment for the stolen goods. As a joke, Veronica asked for his firstborn child, but he apparently did not pick up on the sarcasm and agreed to it without a second thought.

Not having a family of her own, Veronica knew it was a ludicrous bargain but took the opportunity and agreed. Realistically speaking, she knew they'd likely back out of the deal, but the day of the baby's birth arrived and without prompting, the man brought the child right over to Veronica's, who took that sweet baby girl into her home and her heart.

At first, everything was perfect for her and her daughter, Angelica. She loved that child far greater than the parents who threw her away for a handful of vegetables. But before long, the townsfolk got restless about the situation. Veronica's reputation kept them at bay for many years, but Angelica's birth parents began spreading rumors that Veronica had cheated them or terrorized them into giving up the child. They loved skimming over their own culpability.

Things got difficult for Veronica and Angelica until they had to move from the home they loved. Packing up her daughter, Veronica searched for a new place for them to settle, but their story traveled with them, pursuing them and poisoning every village, growing into a monster of fiction. Some claimed Veronica stole the child. Others said she enchanted the wife to crave the plant in the first place and that the cravings were so strong it drove her mad. Others said Veronica was crazy and bit off the fingers of children.

When Angelica was twelve, the townsfolk tried to steal her away and return her to the people who had traded her for a few handfuls of greenery, and Veronica decided the only thing she could do was to hide them both away from the prying interference of neighbors. She found a stretch of lonely woods and built her and Angelica a new home far away from those cruel townsfolk.

Actually, tower is a more apt description than home. It was tall, providing them with a beautiful view, and had only one entrance and exit out the top that was accessible by ladder, giving them distance from the town gossips and fear-mongers. All in all, it wasn't a bad place to live, though a bit too extreme and isolated for my tastes.

Years passed, and mother and daughter lived a happy life until the day a spoiled prince ruined it all. Tricking Angelica into letting him into the tower while Veronica was away, he wooed the poor, sheltered girl and took her to bed before Angelica even understood what was happening. Not that Angelica stood much of a chance when a suave, charismatic princeling turned on his charms; it was like a moth to a flame.

Confident in her impenetrable fortress, Veronica never suspected Angelica had a secret visitor. Too late, Veronica figured it out when the naive girl made a comment to her mother about how tight her dresses were getting. Angelica didn't understand, but Veronica did. Angelica was pregnant.

Veronica moved her daughter out of the tower and away from the prince, but Angelica's mind had been poisoned by his fine words and false heart. He'd learned about Angelica's history and relayed all the horrible lies the people of the realm said about her mother. Angelica ran away to find the idiot prince.

Veronica and I searched for Angelica. We heard rumor that she and the prince had a set of twins and rode off into the sunset to live happily ever after, but we never found any evidence of that. I know the prince married someone else. Once he discovered Angelica wasn't a damsel in distress, he had no interest in her, except as a plaything. Angelica vanished, and neither Veronica nor I have been able to locate the poor girl.

Veronica's best intentions were undone because her fortress wasn't strong enough. Though her walls were tall and thick, the person manning the entrance let the enemy inside. Never allow your plans to be overturned because a hero stumbles through the wrong doorway at the wrong time.

Dungeons

A word on dungeons—don't have one. Ever. Your architect may want to put one in. You may want to put one in. It may feel incomplete without one, but you must stay strong and resist the urge. They look amazing and intimidate your underlings, but they are ridiculous. When you are battling a hero, where is the last place you want them? In your inner sanctum. And where is your dungeon? Do you get the picture? All your security measures mean nothing if you march the captured hero straight past them.

If you don't understand that logic, it's best you shut this book and walk away. There's not a whole lot I can do for you if you can't comprehend this simple yet often overlooked wisdom.

Even keeping it as some sort of fortress accessory isn't a good idea. Its sad and lonely state will be a siren's call to you. Either because of an overwhelming sense of cockiness or boredom, eventually you will break and use your dungeon. Regardless of how secure you feel in your guards or the big locks on the barred doors, heroes are excruciatingly resourceful when it comes to escaping. They always get out.

If you have the hero within your power and absolutely feel the need not to dispose of him immediately (big mistake), keep them held at an off-site facility. It may feel less villainous, but if properly used, it will have the same desired effect.

If you need a reminder on how bad dungeons are for villains, re-read Catherine's story (see "Why Do I Want to Do This?" section of Chapter Two). Though a powerful fairy, she chose to take her enemy into her fortress, and when he escaped he made sure she would never recapture him again.

Decorations

Once you have the fortress built or purchased, it's time to decorate. I'm not suggesting that I have any knowledge or skill with decorating. To be honest, I don't care about the look of a room, but this issue of decorating comes up so frequently with my clients, I feel it necessary to mention it.

Decorations are another place where villains fall into the trap of stereotypes. They want their fortress to be a clear message of villainy to everyone within seven leagues of it. They want it to stand as a beacon of villainy, so they insist on a feel that is generally described as dark, dank, and dreary.

First, I have no idea why anyone would want to live that way. You may be a villain, but you still want a comfortable living space. There's nothing wrong with enjoying a sunny atmosphere with overstuffed chairs and comfy pillows. Working and living in a stereotype is not a pleasant experience. Second, dark, dank, and dreary causes a multitude of avoidable problems.

Fortresses are meant to be your home and/or base of operations. It does not have to be your villainous calling card to the neighbors. Evil lairs draw in heroes, not to mention cost a lot of money to properly outfit. Gargoyles are great, but they will not be fighting alongside your minions, and spending precious funds on things that do nothing to further your plans is ridiculous.

In the end, most of my suggestions for the proper decorating of a fortress can be boiled down to whether you want effect or effectiveness. Shattered windows and dimly lit corridors may be spooky, but they are horribly ineffective. A broken window provides no security from intruders or the elements, and poorly lit rooms are useless for anything but providing the perfect cover for sneaky heroes. If you want to be a villain, keep your fortress properly lit, clean, and organized. If you want people to simply think you are terrifying, keep the darkened corridors and enjoy your inevitable demise. It won't be quick or painless.

And again, here's an area where going against stereotype can be helpful. If a hero gets past your walls and into your inner sanctum only to find it decorated with plush furniture and cheery art, the hero may conclude he was mistaken about you.

A note about pests: there are some villains (especially stepmothers) who allow their fortresses to be infested with animals. They may seem harmless, but while these mice and birds may never do more than squeak or chirp in your presence, they'll burst into song and become unbelievably industrious when a hero or heroine need them. They may seem like brainless vermin, but they're brilliant at aiding heroes and heroines in their schemes or providing useful tidbits of information that inevitably lead to your downfall. Animal control exists for a reason. Use it.

Chapter Six

Outside Help

U nless you are a very small scale villain, you will need help from outside sources. Few villains are successful on their own, and even the smallest plan run smoother if you have the aid of a qualified specialist. You can't do everything alone. Nor should you.

Help can come in different ways, but the most notable are employees and contractors. While others may argue that employees and contractors are the same, there is a significant difference between them. Both play separate roles and have their own strengths and weaknesses.

Employees

Anyone who works exclusively for you is your employee. Period. There's no real need to distinguish too much between the various types of employees you may or may not need. In the end, they're all in your employ. They have one boss and only one boss. You are the one to whom they answer, and the one who controls their career.

However, they come with major issues you need to consider before taking them on. Namely, morale. If employees aren't happy they'll quit. Or more likely, turn on you. If the first happens, your operations will be halted while you scramble to find a replacement. If the second happens, you'll scramble to keep yourself from being executed by a hero.

While employees are especially appealing to the Overlord or anyone else suffering the need for accolades, please be careful. Employees are not your admirers, worshippers, or mindless slaves. They're people who need a paycheck. There may be some company loyalty, and they may even love their work, but in the end, they're there for themselves.

Most villains espouse the belief that they don't have to maintain good relations with those they're paying, and they're absolutely wrong. Monetary compensation is all well and good, but it's not a magic wand. If you expect help with your plans, you have to know how to deal with people. Most people working for villains will struggle with their conscience; you may have a plan that won't hurt a single person while rewarding you and your employees handsomely, but there will still be those in your employ who will wrestle with the decision to be on the "bad guy's" team.

Luckily, most moral compasses don't point due north, and people are willing to toss it out if the price is right. The thing to remember is that each employee has an individual threshold. It's a point where the compensation isn't enough to make them ignore their conscience anymore, and they will turn on you.

Think back to Suzanne (see "Focus" section of Chapter Two). She'd reached her goal of becoming the queen of a country, but more than her vanity and pride got in the way of her maintaining that success. She made the fatal mistake of believing her employee shared her moral standards. Wanting to kill her more beautiful stepdaughter, she sent her huntsman, of all people, to do the job. I don't know why she chose a huntsman instead of an actual assassin, but since she's no longer with us, we'll never know. The huntsman wasn't emotionally equipped to handle the thought of killing a young, attractive (emphasis on attractive) girl.

Do not presume that a paid employee will obey all your orders blindly. As a villain and a boss, part of your job is to make sure they never reach that threshold. That's not done through money, but by maintaining a good relationship. It will not only allow you to know how far you can push them, but it will strengthen their bond to you. If they sympathize with you or like you, the money won't be the only driving force for keeping them way below their personal moral threshold and firmly in your camp.

Money is a necessary motivator, but the stronger one is likability. Be nice to your employees. Treat them fairly. Don't make them hate you because once they hate you, they'll hate your plans and their moral threshold drops. If they like you and like working for you, they'll be far less likely to ever reach the threshold because they'll refuse to believe you're a villain or they'll justify your actions to make them fit comfortably under the employee's moral threshold.

Never underestimate the power of justification. People can talk themselves into doing things they'd never do otherwise.

And maintaining a good relationship with your employees doesn't take much.

Rule #1
Don't ever use death as a punishment

Impending death may seem like a good motivator, but that's the stereotype in you talking. Though you're a villain, you're also a boss, and you have other ways of keeping employees in line other than killing them. Like firing. Villains tend towards violence too often when simpler options are much more effective. Never, ever kill employees. Or their families. Or their puppies. Just don't. Employees don't work well in environments where impending death as a form of punishment is an option.

This rule really should just be, "Don't punish employees". Period. The only reasons for punishing someone is to either A) correct their behavior or B) get retribution. For A, you're not their parent. It's not your job to make them better people. For B, if you need to get retribution from every employee that makes a mistake, you're far too petty to make a good villain. Even a Punisher shouldn't be that childish.

Rule #2
Variety of opinions should be celebrated, not punished

"Yes men" will be the death of you. They only care about their paycheck and keeping their job. They don't care about your success. They're generally the first to jump ship if a better offer comes along.

If you have an employee who points out a fatal flaw in your plans, listen, realistically evaluate it, and fix it or move on. At no point should you ever use the phrase, "That's not possible!" Strike it from your lexicon. With magic, anything is possible, and ignoring the advice of those who are in the trenches is arrogant and self-defeating.

In fact, I would suggest rewarding that employee. They came forward in order to help perfect your plans. That's a sign that they care about the success of your operation. There are those who speak up because they're control freaks who want to be in charge, but most of the time, they say something because they want to help make things better. That attitude should be promoted not exterminated.

Killing people with better ideas is idiotic. Rather than punishing, celebrate their creativity and initiative. This will not only strengthen your plans, but increase employee morale and increase their emotional investment in your plans. It's harder for them to believe your plans are evil if they helped create them.

Rule #3
Be loyal to them and they'll be loyal to you

Like you, employees are human, and they make mistakes. If you have an employee with a good record, don't automatically punish them for one offense—no matter how big it is. Take a moment to talk to them one-on-one and find out if it was incompetence or just human error. Or maybe they were asked to do something for which they aren't qualified, like Suzanne calling on her huntsman to kill her stepdaughter.

If you have an employee making lots of mistakes, it may be that they're in the wrong position. Work with them and see if you can find them a better suited situation. Doing so will earn you stronger loyalty than you could ever buy. Besides, if you hired the wrong person for the wrong job, the blame lies on your head. Firing the employee for your mistake is too close to breaking Rule #2.

Often, employees are blamed for things beyond their control. Doing so will not inspire loyalty among the ranks. And public humiliation never helps the situation.

Loyalty may not seem like a necessity, but paying someone doesn't mean they'll work their hardest or that they will remain on your side. Money guarantees they'll show up and put their time in; happiness guarantees they'll do their best.

Beyond making sure they're satisfied with their positions and not likely to turn on you, you have to be careful about the quality of employees you hire. Too often villains end up with employees who are unprofessional; they run at the first sign of trouble or may cause trouble that attracts heroes. To say nothing of general incompetence. If you hire the wrong employees, you'll end up with bigger troubles.

For example, Jacob was a tailor of little skill or renown in a tiny village in the middle of nowhere. He had little to his name and hoped to move beyond living in the same hovel as his parents in a dead-end job that held little promise of steady income.

His journey into villainy was accidental. When making breakfast one morning, the jam on his toast attracted a number of flies. Not wishing to share his breakfast, he slammed a hand down on the table and smashed seven flies all at once, which his parents thought a grand accomplishment. That might seem strange to you, but I can tell you from personal experience that when your days are spent doing nothing but menial labor and you manage five minutes to relax and entertain yourself but have nothing more to do than staring at dirt on your floor, such mundane events can be counted as momentous.

His parents found it so incredible that they bragged about it to their neighbors, who thought that significantly more interesting than staring at their own dirt floors. Pretty soon, the village knew him as "Seven at One Blow" Jacob. Personally, Jacob didn't understand the fuss. Especially when they presented him a belt embroidered with "Seven at One Blow" across it in big, bold letters.

Which was monumentally awkward. Being talked about for weeks on end was embarrassing enough but giving him a meticulously made present to commemorate such a non-event made it far worse. With no way around hurting his friends and family, Jacob strapped it on and that moment set him on the path that landed him on my doorstep.

As I've mentioned previously, heroes and non-villains aren't terribly bright and tend to take what they see at face value, regardless of the improbability. While on a trip to a nearby village, people saw Jacob's belt and inferred it to mean he was a serious warrior. Instead of flies (because what weirdo would brag about that), they assumed the "Seven at One Blow" meant he'd killed seven men. Since he wasn't ugly or dressed in black, people thought him a great adventurer who'd accomplished some grand heroic deed.

Before long, Jacob crossed paths with a giant who wanted to prove he was much stronger than the tiny Jacob—seven men killed in one blow or not. Luckily, Jacob saw an opportunity when it presented itself, and he used his brain to best the giant.

That's when Jacob approached me. He saw the possibility of turning this mistaken reputation into a serious blessing for him and his family.

Using his reputation and heroic appearance, we landed Jacob a position far higher up the social and financial ladder than being the younger son of a poor village tailor. As a member of the Royal Guards in a nearby kingdom, Jacob was introduced to the king, who recognized a fellow villain. You see, the king was no more a hero than Jacob was. He'd tricked and villained his way to the top and had no interest in being usurped by an upstart villain.

Enticing Jacob with promises of the princess's hand in marriage and being named heir to the throne, the king sent Jacob on a seemingly impossible quest. What the king didn't realize was that Jacob wasn't alone in his endeavors. With my resources on his side, Jacob easily conquered it. Of course, the king threw another at him. Which Jacob defeated. And still a third quest was thrown his way. As each challenge came up, the king got more desperate, finally sending his soldiers after Jacob to stop him, but the king didn't have great taste in employees and they failed each and every time.

Finally, the king conceded and allowed Jacob his reward. Of course, that didn't last long. Though the king knew the truth about Jacob, his daughter thought him a true hero. When she found out her new husband was only an opportunistic tailor, she went to her father and demanded he get rid of Jacob. Not having learned his lesson before, the king agreed and sent a group of his best soldiers to kill Jacob in his sleep.

However, the king didn't understand the importance of quality employees. He had a supremely unhappy squire in his employ. I don't know why nor do I care, but the fact was that while the king thought his employees loyal, his squire snuck behind his back and warned Jacob of what was coming.

To add insult to managerial injury, the king discovered his best soldiers were cowards. When they arrived at Jacob's room to take him to the chopping block, he simply blustered about, laying claim to all the rumors of his heroic deeds and strength. By now stories of his "heroism" were so widespread that though the soldiers had never seen any real example of strength or fighting prowess, they believed every single one of Jacob's lies and ran for the hills.

After that, the king and princess couldn't muster up the backbone to try again, and the tailor has since been made king of the country and rules happily. And safely. None of the neighboring kingdoms dare attack the kingdom ruled by a man who can kill seven with one blow.

If the king had been better staffed, Jacob and I would have moved on to a new plan, but he trusted weak employees and lost his kingdom. If your plans relies on the capability and help of other people, make sure you choose the right people.

If you're struggling to find quality employees, please contact the Ward Employment Agency. Separate from Ward Villainy Consulting, WEA provides quality minions at reasonable rates. Yes, I am self-promoting, but what are you going to do about it?

Contractors

Contractors are a different breed from employees. They are highly skilled in their individual area and thus tend to be more expensive than an average employee. Because of that expense, few can afford to keep them on staff permanently, so contractors work on individual projects for multiple villains at a time. I consider them separate because they have different benefits and weaknesses than an employee.

Expense is generally the only downside to contractors. They know their work, and they're good at it, so you're going to have to pay for their level of skill.

However, they do not have the moral or morale issues of employees. Contractors know what they were hired for and why. They're professional on a much higher level. They have their contract and will fulfill it. You do have to be careful about who you get into business with, but as long as you hire a reputable contractor, you won't have to worry.

Frankly, I don't see the need to further convince you

with grand examples, as this book is already chock full of them. In case you haven't figured it out, I'm a contractor. You hire me to get you to the top, but I do not work for you. We work together. If you need more convincing as to why you need contractors at times, feel free to flip to the front of this manual and read it again.

Chapter Seven

You and Your Loved Ones

No villain exists in a bubble, and part of your success will lie in dealing with the non-villains in your life. In my experience, most relationships cause more problems than they are worth. Friends, parents, girlfriends/boyfriends, spouses, children, and all the like hinder your progress more often than not.

They may care about you and vice versa, but the public prejudice against villains is so rampant that most likely they will not understand or support the path you've chosen for yourself. Keeping people in your life who do not support you and your decisions will make it all that more difficult to achieve your goals. Keeping anything in your life that thwarts your plans is self-destructive.

If you keep "loved" ones in your life because you are

lonely, you have a bigger problem. Like I mentioned previously, looking for recognition or validation from others never works. People rarely give us the reaction we crave.

Public opinion is so swayed against villains that though most of us don't do anything particularly evil, people will assume your heart is black as pitch—regardless of how unwicked your intensions. Lifelong friends and beloved family disowned me when I stepped from the hero to the villain path. It didn't matter that I only did so to avoid marrying a total harpy of a princess, the minute I refused my heroic destiny, I became a villain.

Being a villain means you will be alone. Sorry if that's disheartening, but you're going after these goals because you want something. If that's love and acceptance, you'd better stay put. You have been duly warned, but read further if you need more convincing.

Friends

Friends are the least complicated of all the types of relationships in your life. You pick your friends; be careful about who you invite into your life, and you'll be fine.

Make sure your friends fully support your villainous decisions both now and in the future. If they waiver at the beginning of your journey, they will inevitably collapse beneath their conscience and side with the heroes or pester you to change your plans.

Regardless of how entertaining the relationship may be, it will cause infinitely more problems if it goes south.

Parents, Siblings, Spouses, and Children

In general, it is better to avoid all these relationships. Families can cause you no end of headaches. It brings into your life an inexplicable indebtedness that can cause roadblocks and hurdles in your villainous endeavors.

Friends you can choose, but your family are biologically linked to you, which may be the one and only thing you have in common with them. If you don't believe me, simply ask my mother. Granted, if you do try to ask her about me, she'll simply slam the door in your face.

My mother had high hopes for my future as a hero. She felt sure I was destined for a grand quest and spent my childhood preparing me for the time when I would leave home to fulfill this destiny. The morning of my eighteenth birthday, my mother celebrated by pulling me from bed and shoving me out the door with only the clothes on my back. My quest led me down a different path than she intended, one which has made her excruciatingly unhappy. She wanted a hero. Not a hero-turned-villain.

For years, she picked and fussed and fumed about my life, trying to force me back onto the path she'd chosen for me. There were times when she almost succeeded. When times are rough and you're struggling to see the light at the end of the tunnel, the last thing you need is someone encouraging you to give up.

When I stood my ground and let her know in no uncertain terms that I wasn't going to be bullied from my career, she promptly cut me from her life, making my own much easier. I still have contact with some of my sisters, but none from my parents. I don't share this to encourage some great swell of pity on your part, but to teach you a valuable lesson. Family is fine and all, but they can end up destroying your plans if you're not careful. You have to decide if they're more important than your life of villainy.

Stepchildren

In general, marriage isn't a good option for villains. Spouses are a weird mix of friend and family with the added drama of romantic love thrown into the mix. But if you choose to move forward with marriage, beware if they have children. The spouse may cause you the general problems that a normal spouse or family member would, but your new stepchildren will likely be your downfall.

Of all the relationships you can have, these are the most dangerous. It is one of the reasons why I enjoy working with stepmothers and stepfathers. They present a more difficult challenge even if their schemes are less flashy than large-scale villains. They may be working in a smaller pond, but their fish are more vicious.

The most common and deadly relationship is that of the stepmother and stepdaughter. Stepdaughters are ruthless. They smile and bat their eyes at the general public with a practiced air of sweetness and innocence, but they are exceptionally vindictive and will do what they can to torture you. And I do not mean only metaphorically; just ask Nicole's stepmother (see "The Counselor" section in Chapter One).

This reminds me of a flower I read about once that is beautiful and unique in its makeup. It sends out sweet scents and paints itself with vibrant colors to attract the insects. However, when the poor little guys crawl inside, the flower snaps shut, trapping the fly inside, slowly digesting it. I have to imagine is not the most pleasant of deaths.

If you are thinking of binding yourself in marriage to someone with a child, proceed with caution. The minute you do, you've invited a hero or heroine into your life, and that is not a battle to enter into lightly. If you are marrying for villainous means, I am certain you can find someone equally suitable who carries less baggage with them.

Though if the stepdaughter in question is unattractive, don't worry. No matter what happens, no prince is coming to rescue her.

If you are already stuck with a stepbrat or two, the best advice I can give you is to treat them better than their natural born parents would. There are ways to get rid of them (most of which would require more hands-on aid than a book can give), but I would generally advise against it. While it is good fun to take on a challenge, it is only for the strongest and craftiest of villains.

It may be tempting to be horrible to them since your spouse will most likely not care, but don't give into temptation. For some reason, the minute you marry, your spouse will ignore what happens to the children. I don't know if it's willing ignorance or heartlessness, but they tend to look the other way when their children are being bullied or hurt by you. Some would argue it's blind love of you, but my own experience tells me it's mostly heartlessness.

A wicked stepmother by the name of Sybyl approach me once. She planned to be a Counselor Villain by pushing her natural born daughter into royal paths. However, neither Sybyl nor her daughter had the beauty to attract a prince. I tried to steer her in a different path, but we couldn't see eye-to-eye on the matter. She moved forward on her own, and I watched from afar as her plans imploded.

Sybyl married a wealthy man to put herself in a position where her daughter could meet the right people. Correction. I should say she extorted a marriage. I'm not sure what she did to secure his hand in matrimony, but I know it wasn't done willingly. That was her second mistake, but not her worst.

The man had two children by his first wife, a boy and a girl. Angry that their beauty made her daughter even uglier by comparison, she picked and bullied the children until she couldn't take it anymore and tried to kill them. Of course, the kids were wilier than she imagined, and they escaped into the woods. She tracked them and tried cursing them twice, but the stepdaughter always saw through the enchantments and saved her and her brother. The third curse hit its mark. Sort of.

Sybyl turned the boy into a deer, hoping he would be killed by hunters, but since the curse missed the girl, she was able to protect her brother at every turn.

Time passed and eventually a king was hunting in the forest and came across the stepdaughter. Instantly entranced by her beauty, he married her at once, ruining Sybyl's plans for her daughter's royal future. Rather than letting it go and moving onto Plan B, Sybyl went after the stepdaughter again.

Using another curse on her stepdaughter/the new queen, Sybyl hit her with a curse that put the girl into a coma. Thinking it a death curse, Sybyl hid the body and disguised her daughter to look like the stepdaughter. Again, better to move to Plan B than to try and force this convoluted mess of a plan.

Of course, it was found out. Death-like curses always allow for massive loopholes in which the heroines can escape, and in this case, her spirit was able to wander ghostlike at night. After a couple visits to various people in the castle, they figured out the truth and did what most sane, rational non-villains do—they fed the daughter to wild beasts in the forest and burned Sybyl at the stake.

If you reject the kindness route, make sure whatever you do to them is final and there is no chance they can ever retaliate. There should not even be a miniscule chance because if there is, your punishment will be far worse than anything you did to them.

Those sweet and "righteous" stepchildren are infinitely more cruel than their "evil" stepparent. Attempted murder is punished with being forced to wear red-hot iron shoes and to dance until you die or being burned at the stake. Forced servitude is punished with death by birds pecking out your eyeballs. And they say villains are cruel.

It is best to avoid stepchildren. It will increase your life expectancy significantly.

Romance

Love can be an incredible motivator. For heroes. Romance and villainy do not work well together. I am not arguing whether or not romance has merit in normal lives— that is for non-villains to debate—I am saying that while you are maintaining a villainous lifestyle, it is imperative to steer clear of the opposite sex if you cannot control yourself.

I have several reasons why I say this.

Firstly, courting is a miserable process that brings you

more stress than joy. Those who claim courting is fun have never been set up on a blind date with Gertrude, the blacksmith's daughter whose hobbies include dressing her pets in a wide variety of outfits and weaving tapestries to capture the fun (or "cat"ture, as she calls it).

At best, you have a little fun in the short term that ends in horrible agony when your relationship dies a slow and agonizing death, which is followed by months, if not years, of awkward run-ins with the person. And that is assuming the other doesn't take the breakup to a more extreme level with weeks of stalking. I have had my fair share of burning effigies left on my doorstep, and I can tell you now that it is not worth it. I heard courting once described as riding in a boat that sinks every time except once. Apt.

By avoiding courting, you will be saving yourself a world of pain when it doesn't work out. And if it does work out, it'll just throw you right into all the issues I mentioned in the section about family.

And before you think to yourself that kidnapping is a viable courtship option, let me put it this way—if you have to kidnap a person to get them to be with you, they don't like you that way. A good time to move on. Kidnapping may be considered a perfectly villainous thing to do, but it's guaranteed to ruin your plans.

Secondly, romance makes you weak. If you keep that door open, if you even allow yourself to muse about the possibility of finding love, you are opening yourself up to the possibility of falling for the dreaded heroines. Both heroes and heroines are dashing and gorgeous, which makes it difficult to keep your blinders on. How else would the heroes and heroines fall "in love" so fast with each other? It is like they are a special breed of human designed to make people fall for them instantly, so they can bewitch their "true love" before they open their mouths and be seen for the twit they are.

When I was a hero, I found a princess at the end of my quest. She was devastatingly beautiful, and I was smitten in an instant. I was convinced I loved her and we were meant to be together. Luckily, it took several days for us to arrive in her kingdom, during which time I realized I wanted to be with her as much as I want to cut off my leg with a rusty saw. She blinded me and almost made me miss my opportunity for true happiness in my current profession.

Heroines are not opposed to using those super gorgeous superpowers to their best advantage. She's a heroine. She stands for everything you are against and vice versa. If she flirts with you, you can bet she has a devious plan in store.

All in all, romance is not a good idea for a villain. If after all I have written, you have even a tiny, miniscule part of your heart telling you I am wrong about this, you need to reevaluate your goals because it sounds as though villainy isn't your tip-top priority. If you want romance and won't close your heart to it, the only way you will find it is by giving up your villainous ways. In which case, put down this book and become a baker. Or mason. Or farmer. Anything other than villain.

Chapter Eight

Dealing with the Masses

It would be remiss of me not to mention a most important relationship—that of the villain and the nameless masses. There are three groups who may or may not affect you success:

1. Those who stand with you
2. Those who stand against you
3. Those who stand on the sidelines

Those who stand with you may be your minions or contractors; anyone who is there to help you on your way. At times, that may include your family and friends (if after you've read the last chapter you still insist on having them). Those who stand against you are obviously the heroes, heroines, and anyone else helping them. Those on the sidelines are everyone else. They're the ones effected by your villainy career but do nothing. They neither fight nor help you.

As I've already discussed members of the first group at length, I won't bother repeating myself. If you need a refresher, I suggest you flip back to Chapter Six. And if you already need a refresher on what you read only two chapters ago, you're not suited for a villain's life. I'll be covering the second group later on, but here I want to discuss the third.

For small scale villains, such as the evil stepmother, this group is almost non-existent. Mostly, your plans involve only you and your stepchild, the prince or king who come into the picture, and your spouse. Since the sphere of people affected by your plans is small, the people you'll need to deal with will be very few. And as I've already mentioned, spouses tend to check out of their kids' lives once they remarry.

For large scale villains, such as a future king or queen, the third group can be a huge problem for you. Those in the third group include anyone in your future kingdom. Though the masses tend not to care about the goings on of the royalty, you will have problems if they are mishandled.

The Movement of the Groups

It may seem strange to dedicate an entire chapter to people who have nothing to do with your plans, but the huddled hordes can cause problems if not treated correctly. Nothing is set in stone with people. Just because they're in a specific group doesn't mean that they can't move into another if given the proper incentives. With enough enticement, members of the third group will slide into the second, joining forces with those who want to bring you down.

The majority of people don't care what villains or heroes do. They are neither allies nor enemies, and as long as you don't severely, negatively affect their everyday life, they will stay firmly rooted in that third group. Villains have a problem when they ignore or abuse that third group, giving them enough motivation to join the second.

The main thing I wish for you to take from this section is this: save your villainy for the heroes. The average person is too busy with their own lives to care what trouble the royals get themselves into or what their neighbor is doing. They are firmly stuck in their own little bubble; as long as you don't pop it, they'll be content to remain so.

Angry townsfolk can be a powerful weapon. One you don't want the hero getting his hands on. From your high and lofty perch, they may seem like unimportant little ants, but they have a surprising tendency to form mobs if not handled carefully.

In Chapter Five, I mentioned Veronica and her daughter Angelica. The birth parents weren't heroes or heroines, but members of the masses. They would have remained so, except the anger at losing their baby pushed them into the group staunchly in favor of stopping Veronica. In turn, they riled up the emotions of the others, pulling others into the fight against Veronica. It drove them from town to town, making it impossible for Veronica to have the happy life she wanted for her daughter. Thus the tower in the middle of nowhere, which didn't end well.

There is no reason to lash out at innocent bystanders.

There's no need to wipe out villages or destroy the lives of random townsfolk. If they're not standing in your way, they don't need your villainous attentions. Trust me, heroes and heroines are enough of an enemy. Not to mention that a lot of future heroes and heroines have loved ones; you never know when you might inadvertently hurt one of them, pushing that dormant hero or heroine into action.

Keep on good terms with the sideliners. Once people are stirred to action, it is impossible for them to go back to being docile. When that change is made, it sticks. So, don't give them any reason to join up with the second group.

And don't bother trying to recruit them to join up with you. You're more often than not going to be simply hurting yourself if they ever turn on you. Which they do. Often. Far too often. It's best to keep your allies list short and sweet. The sheep of group three aren't worth the effort.

Really, it comes down to the fact that once people are in group two, they don't move out of it. If you've angered your allies, they don't just wander off and do nothing, they join up with the hero. Once angry enough to act, the peasants won't just go back to not caring.

Once you've made an enemy, they're your enemy for good.

That's not to say you can't exploit the peasants to a degree. Just be smart about it. If you take everything away from them, it gives them a reason to care about what you're doing. If you exact high taxes but not too high, you'll get grumbling, but that's where it will end. You don't have to make them happy, but moderately disgruntled peasants don't form rebellions or uprisings or produce heroes. Frankly, most peasants are always moderately disgruntled.

Do not taunt peasants with your wealth. Don't hold

lavish banquets or balls during a famine. In fact, avoid doing anything that can be described as "lavish" when your underlings are starving. Poor people don't often realize how poor they are until it's shoved in their face. As long as they're blissfully ignorant about how good you have it compared to their lives, they won't bother lighting the torches or gathering the pitchforks.

Poverty is relative. They may be much better off than the next kingdom over, but if they see you sitting on your throne with a big ol' turkey leg in your hand, surrounded by piles of jewels, they'll feel entitled to more. It won't matter if their standard of living is much higher than other kingdoms; what they will see is you having more than them. People never grow up. Childhood tactics are alive and well and important to remember. If one of the other children see you with a piece of candy, they'll want it—regardless of what they may have.

Just remember, having a legion of highly trained soldiers at your back doesn't mean you are all-powerful. Brute strength is no guarantee of victory. And if you don't believe that, remember how you were able to overthrow your predecessor.

A Lifetime of Vigilance

Even after your plans have come to fruition and you've become high ruler of all you survey, you still have to be weary of that third group. Years from now some brat may grow up to overthrow you. Being a villain attracts heroes. The longer you are an open, public villain, the more chances a hero will show up and beat you.

I knew a hero named Guy who was so dimwitted that he'd often forget his own but he stopped a villain who'd held his own against much more formidable heroes over the years. Guy was the younger son of some peasant from somewhere; I never did get a straight answer out of him about who his father was or where he came from, but that doesn't matter in the context of the story.

He was a nice enough kid but definitely a few apples short of a pie. His father wanted him to learn a trade, but Guy didn't get the concept and decided his father meant him to learn a skill. Any skill. Thinking over his life, Guy choose a skill he deemed most useful—how to shudder. I kid you not. Guy had heard others talk about being scared so much they would shudder. He'd never felt that before and thought it was about time he did.

I've never gotten a clear understanding about what happened next, I do know that a neighbor found out about it and wanted to mess with Guy, so the neighbor pretended to be a ghost or some monster. Rather than scaring Guy like he had planned, Guy attacked the "monster", pushing him either down the stairs or out the window. Either way, the neighbor broke his leg, causing a bit of trouble in the village. Villagers' loyalties change faster than the wind, and the slightest thing can get them grabbing their pitchforks and torches. So, Guy's family announced it was high time for him to go out into the world on his own.

Eventually, he came to another town where the townsfolk found out about Guy's quest. Being bored and poor, they decided the best way to entertain themselves was to mess with Guy. According to him, the townsfolk had him spend the night outside with seven men who were so stupid they would not speak. They didn't have any coats, so he invited them to share his fire, but they got too close and set their clothes on fire, so he sent them away.

Strange story, but when I dug a little deeper, I got the full story from the townsfolk. They had him spend the night under a gallows, where seven men had been hung the day before. The "stupid" men who didn't have coats were the corpses, which he cut down and brought to the fire. When they caught fire, he decided they were too stupid to be worth his time, and he hung them back where he had found them.

And Guy still didn't know how to shudder. If he'd been a villain and a client of mine, I would have warned him that a better lesson to learn was how to use that brain of his. But it worked out for him in the end.

He moved on to the next town, where there was a castle with a psycho cannibal living in it. They called him a monster, which he certainly was but not in a physical sense. The monster wasn't a beast or creature. He was a man, though everyone convinced themselves he was some magical being who could separate his legs from his body. I do think he may have been a sorcerer of some sort, but past that, not a lot is known about him.

The monster (I shudder to call him a villain because he was more psychopath than villain) had taken over the castle, killing off its inhabitants and any hero who came looking for trouble. The monster stirred up enough trouble that the nearby king offered a massive reward and his daughter's hand in marriage to anyone who defeated it. When Guy showed up in the kingdom, the villagers pointed him towards the monster, and he went straight into its lair.

The monster had been especially good at playing off the fears of his victims, using it in his own sadistic way to make them easy prey. But Guy wasn't afraid of anything because he didn't understand anything. For two nights, the monster tormented him, but Guy laughed it all off, thinking it was a game. Eventually, it was the monster who slipped up, and Guy took the upper hand. Though how the fool realized it when it came, I'll never know. Guy killed the monster, took over the castle, and married the fair princess.

Because the monster/villain/psychopath hurt and maimed a lot of people, it drew attention. Even though he had beaten hundreds of heroes before Guy, he failed in the end. It doesn't matter how many times you win if you lose your life. One fail is all it takes to overturn a lifetime of success.

Decoys Are Our Friends

I've mentioned that the line between hero and villain is hazy and that line gets even more distorted by the fact that the stories told of villains are created by whoever is left standing. The best way for you to survive long after you've achieved your plans is to write the story in a way that makes you look good.

Even if at first everyone acknowledges you were a villain, if the story is twisted to make you look better and is told enough times, people eventually forget your less heroic origins. You become the hero that saved them.

Anger is like having an irritable dragon on your hands. Trying to calm it is impossible, and there's little in the world, outside of magic, that can block their fiery breath. So, get it to turn its head away. Redirecting anger is much easier than diffusing it.

Give the peasants a good enough yarn, and they'll run

with it. Future heroes won't think to usurp your power if they believe you were a hero who overcame a nefarious villain. I've shared many examples in this manual where that has been the case, but I'll indulge myself by sharing another. Mostly, because it's funny how the story has gotten so twisted over the years.

Several years ago, a friend of mine asked for help. He was terminally ill and afraid for the three boys he was leaving behind. The economy crashed a couple years before, leaving him only enough to provide for the eldest two. His youngest, poor John, had nothing, and my friend had little time left to do anything for him.

Frantic about his son's prospects, he asked me to help John in exchange for a pair of boots. That might sound like a strange trade, but they were a family heirloom. I've been told they were magic at one point, though I doubt there's even a spark in them anymore. Regardless, they've never scuffed or shown an ounce of wear and tear in the years I have worn them. Not to mention they're the most comfortable boots I've ever worn. Definitely worth the trade.

Back to the point. Royalty are not always the brightest and most capable in the land, and sometimes trickery works much better than forcing them to bend to your will.

The first stage of my plan involved sending a gift to a nearby king. I knew he had a fondness for rabbits, which were plentiful around John's home but rare in the other kingdom. So, I caught a brace and took them to the king, claiming them to be a present from the Marquis of Cadwallader. As there are too many royals in the world to count, the king simply accepted the gift, pleased to have such a delicacy from his new friend.

Then I only had to get John in the path of the king, but

his clothing wasn't up to royal standards. This was early on in my career, and I didn't have the liquid funds to outfit John, so we had to be a little creative.

After finding out that the king was going to be traveling by a certain lake, I had John jump in the water and pretend to drown. When the royal coach passed, I stopped them and begged them to save my Lord and Master the Marquis of Cadwallader. And yes, calling him my Lord and Master made me sick to my stomach. Calling anyone produces a strong gag reflex.

Recognizing the name of his rabbit supplier, the king stopped, had his men rescue John, and dressed him in the king's spare clothes; we told them thieves had stolen John's clothes and thrown him in the lake, and the king didn't bat an eye at that. Nor did he ask why I didn't save him myself. Since I was in the role of manservant, the king didn't have high expectations for my abilities.

Once John was dressed in finery, the royals didn't hesitate to accept John as one of their own. The princess was dazzled, and they set off on their way with Lord John in tow. Heading down the road, we stopped at various intervals. When the local peasants were asked whose land the king was on, they each replied, "The Marquis of Cadwallader's". It took only a few strategic bribes to get the peasants' cooperation, and we had the king and princess convinced that the vast estates we'd been traveling across were all John's.

They arrived at a large estate that John claimed was his. It actually belonged to another client of mine (who let us borrow it while he was on vacation), but the king and princess didn't know any better. In their eyes the borrowed estate was in reality John's, who was an honest to goodness royal, like them.

The king was convinced that John was a royal. The daughter was convinced she was head-over-heels in love with John. John was convinced we were going to be caught and strung up in a giblet. But I knew better.

After a few glasses of wine, the king offered John the princess's hand in marriage, and John's future was fixed. After the wedding, when the king discovered the truth, he wasn't happy but wasn't unhappy about getting his single daughter off his hands; the king certainly had holdings and riches enough to compensate for John's lack.

The story of their romance spread far and wide, stretching and changing, as stories do. The funny thing is that in essence it has remained the same. Story John is a peasant who tricks his way into a royal marriage. But the author behind his rise to power isn't the dreaded villainy consultant. It's a magic cat.

You see, a magic cat obviously isn't evil and wouldn't help a villain. He's something akin to a fairy godmother for men. The story has twisted enough that people accept that it's a heroic story. John isn't a villain, he's a hero to the point that even his wife and father-in-law view him as such.

The point is that the fickle masses can be easily swayed to believe something different. Twist together a good story, and they'll redirect their anger onto another target. You become the hero, and your fallen enemy, the villain.

Chapter Nine

Heroes

I t may seem strange that I've waited so long to analyze heroes, but getting yourself in order is a higher priority. If you've learned and applied the lessons from the earlier chapters, the chances of you encountering a hero will be slimmer. And if you haven't straightened yourself out, you have no chance against them. In fact, though the next couple chapters are important, I would suggest spending more time studying the earlier ones.

As a note, villainous men and women can be described jointly as villains. They aren't viewed separately by the heroes and the same rules apply to both. The same is not true about heroes and heroines. For clarity's sake, I will be speaking about them separately. Heroines will be address in the next chapter.

The Heroes Regime

Where villains have a wide range of backgrounds, heroes have rigid rules dictating who is a hero and how they can be heroic. Frankly, that's why most villains exist. Yes, amateur Havockers may only like being villainous for the sake of villainy, but as a whole, villains are predefined by the heroes as any who are fighting the heroic status quo.

Heroes fall into two classes: the prince and the pauper. In the hero's world, there's no room for anything between. Princes require only a title to be a hero. They're generally considered good looking (whether it's true or the title blinding people is up for debate), but they aren't a terribly intelligent group as a whole. Yes, you'll find the odd prince who has two brain cells to rub together, but mostly they're spoiled and coddled laze-abouts.

On the other hand, paupers have a moderate amount of backstory leeway. They may include huntsmen, woodcutters, farmers, millers, tailors, and the like. Princes are attributed all sorts of abilities by nature of their title (bravery, attractiveness, etc.), but paupers must actually have those heroic qualities. Looks are important, but they must be intelligent and brave. As paupers aren't blessed at birth with great resources, they've got to work ten times harder to achieve the same level of heroic success. Do not underestimate the power behind paupers. They may not have the instant prestige and money of the princes, but they are a scrappy bunch who can cause just as much trouble.

One of my first clients was a man by the name of Derrick. Frankly, I look back at it and wonder what we were both thinking, but we were young and new in our fields.

Like me, Derrick was a former hero, but unlike me, he came from a royal background. As a younger son of a king, he had no responsibilities. With the heir, the spare, and several more brothers between him and the throne, he had nothing to do but head off on a hero's quest. Following his assigned path, he neared the finish line. But just before he rescued the fair maiden, he did what no other prince I've known has done—he thought.

People may think that heroes get the prize in the end, but when the prize is marriage to a self-important spoiled brat, I can tell you that it is no prize at all. He took one look at his future and realized it wasn't what he wanted. Of course, you can't not marry a princess at the end and survive with your reputation intact, so he was forced into finding another life for himself.

When our paths crossed, he intrigued me. A prince who rejects being a prince is always worth looking into. We got talking, and he shared his grand scheme. He knew of other royals who wanted to start their marriage with more than a passing acquaintance with their spouse and a great story about how they met. He wanted to provide a way to court without the inconvenience of their parents' disapproval. After all, meeting your groom or bride when one of you hasn't been cursed or kidnapped just isn't done.

He wanted to create a secret royal courting service. Though I don't care about royals finding love (since they already get everything else), I do approve of anyone being able to choose the path for their lives, which is how I got wrapped up in this scheme.

We created a special system of enchanted tunnels connecting Derrick's clients to his base of operations. For a fee, his clients would be given access to the entrances, which opened at specified times. Every night Derrick threw lavish parties and balls where his clients could gather together, meet other singles, and dance the night away. It was the perfect set-up. He raked in money, and his clients were able to date before they married.

At the time, I thought it was a perfect scheme. Looking back, I realized I should have known better; whenever heroines are involved, heroes are sure to follow.

Before long, whispers and rumors circulated about a royal family with several daughters enrolled in Derrick's service. Besides not being smart enough to hide the evidence (such as their worn dancing shoes), they were so desperate to marry, they tired themselves out night after night. It didn't take long before the kingdom noticed things weren't right with the princesses. The girls developed a habit of falling asleep at the most inappropriate times. The bubble-headed twits weren't even smart enough to come up with plausible lies for their parents. They simply refused to answer any questions, which only added fuel to the fire.

Derrick, the big softy, didn't have the heart to cut them as clients and despite my suggestions, focused on trying to help the girls get around their parents' safeguards. He may have claimed to be a villain, but the guy had a weakness for distraught princesses.

Unable to get the girls to give them a straight answer, their parents set guards to figure out what happened to them, but Derrick gave the girls a drug that knocked out the guards.

With all the mystery surrounding the girls, the heroes started arriving, determined to save the princesses from the mysterious enchantment holding them captive. Luckily, Derrick was no fool and knew how to deal with the heroes.

He kept a close eye on the situation and dealt with each issue. Soon, the number of princes thinned, and Derrick felt confident that he'd outwitted them.

That's when the pauper hero showed up.

Derrick wouldn't listen to me. I warned him that they were scrappier and smarter than the average prince, but being a former prince himself, Derrick took immediate offense. Things fell apart from there.

The hero was a poor soldier returning from war, which should have set off all sorts of alarms for Derrick. The pauper was trained in all sorts of subterfuge and fighting, but Derrick wouldn't listen. It took only a couple days for the soldier to figure out the entire scheme and expose it, uprooting all of Derrick's plans.

I will say Derrick handled it right in the end. When everything was found out and the royal guards swarmed the ball, he simply faded into the group of royal clients, all of whom claimed they were there due to an enchantment. Never being exposed as the mastermind behind the plot, Derrick didn't face punishment at the hero's hand. In fact, he married one of the princesses he met during his scheme, so even though his plans fell to pieces, he got something out of it.

Understanding the difference between the prince and the pauper not only helps clarify what you're up against, but it can help identify what kind of hero you're dealing with.

The Rescuer

This is the most common of all the types of hero, and they tend to be exceptionally generic. So generic that even when tales of their heroism are spread far and wide, they're generally known as simply "the prince" or "the king" or the incredibly vacuous "Prince Charming". There are so many "Prince Charmings" that it's impossible to keep them straight. Or, it simply could be a single guy who is a prolific polygamist, but princes are a dime a dozen and Rescuers tend to blend together, so I'd say that's less likely.

Rescuers are almost entirely royalty. Most princes view it as their royal duty to rescue maidens, and I would say the majority of princes take on this heroic role. There are exceptions, but pauper Rescuers are rare. Derrick's case is a prime example. Paupers are never called on to rescue maidens (especially princesses) until the princes are done trying. My own heroic journey followed that rule. I was a pauper who rescued a fair maiden, but only after everyone royal had given up.

The Rescuer is only interested in saving the fair damsel in distress. That's it. He doesn't care about anything past riding off into the sunset with his bride-to-be, and not always that; sometimes it's just the rescue that they want, but they're stuck with the girl. And even though it is the most common hero, it is also the easiest to avoid because the Rescuer's focus is so tight. If there's no heroine to Rescue, they'll never bother you. So, don't involve a heroine and you're fine.

If your plans specifically involve some silly heroine, and you absolutely cannot see any other way to achieve your goals without it and are determined to move forward, you better ready your escape plan or funeral. Once Rescuers get involved, they are impossible to defeat. Rescuers may not be incredibly crafty or quick witted, but they tend to attract magical help by the barrelful. It's like magical creatures can't help themselves when they see a lovesick hunk pining for his lady fair. Magic will intervene, and you will fail.

One way to mitigate the Rescuer is to keep the heroine far away from you. Generally, heroes don't seek out villains for retribution; if you're out of their line of sight when they rescue the heroine, then you should survive. Once they ride into the sunset, they tend to consider their story over, and they won't bother you.

Another way is to make the hero and heroine believe someone else is the villain. Like in Charles's story, where he married an evil stepmother to take the blame for his villainy (see "The Counselor" section of Chapter One). Charles faked a coma, took himself out of the equation, and left the evil stepmother and daughter to cause the heroine trouble. Once the hero became involved, both the heroine and the hero believe the evil stepmother and stepdaughters were the one who carried the blame. This is difficult to pull off and shouldn't be considered lightly.

Luckily, I haven't lost many clients this way, but I've heard a fair many stories that ended tragically because of a Rescuer. I know of a queen by the name of Magdalena who had used all her womanly wiles to con her way into power. Frankly, it sounds like she did well for herself if you figure she did so completely on her own and with no magical or consultary aid. However, if Magdalena had someone in her corner, they would have told her to leave it alone when her stepson showed up one day with a new wife and kids in tow.

Apparently, they married secretly years before when the girl awoke from a sleeping curse. Don't ask me why it was secret; I've never gotten a straight answer out of the guy, but I get the feeling he wanted to maintain his bachelor lifestyle but felt obligated to marry the girl after he Rescued her. But that's neither here nor there.

Much to Magdalena's shock and dismay, the prince had decided it was time to admit his marriage to the public. His father had died, and it was time for him to ascend the throne. Instead of accepting that all good things must come to an end, she decided to get rid of the new queen and her children.

Of course, the story goes that Magdalena was a half-ogre who ordered the court chef to cook the children and serve them for dinner, but I doubt that's true. Besides the fact that she wasn't half-anything, I have a hard time believing anyone savvy enough to reach Magdalena's position would be silly enough to do something so ostentatious. But I have heard of stranger and stupider things. Anything is possible, though I don't think that sounds like Magdalena. It sounds more like the lies of a vindictive hero and heroine.

According to the story, the chef pretended to cook the kids, but Magdalena found out and took matters into her own hands and decided tossing them in a pit of poisonous snakes and spiders would be an effective assassination. Again, ridiculous.

Just as she was going to toss in the kids and queen, the king Rescued his family and pushed Magdalena inside.

I'm not sure how much of this is true, and I doubt anyone other than the king and queen know what really happened to Magdalena, but the end result is the same. The king and queen got their happily ever after, and Magdalena died.

Rescuers love to swoop in and save the day. If they do so, you will lose more than your victory. The best thing you can do is not attract their attention in the first place. If you are unfortunate as to attract one, drop everything and run. Run as far and fast as you can. At least that way you'll survive.

The Adventurer

The Adventurers are the thrill seeking heroes sometimes known as Questers. They want the adventure, the rush of heading into the unknown. Because of that, they're the most unpredictable of the heroes. They don't have a solid purpose to their wanderings other than popping into your life to cause you nothing but headaches.

The Adventurers skew more towards paupers than princes. Princes spend their days looking for princesses, but the farm boys, millers, and tailors search for excitement. I was an Adventurer. Granted, my mother shoved me out the door, but it was the thrill that kept my feet heading down that path.

The best way to keep Adventurers out of your plans is to make yourself uninteresting. Don't establish an aura of mystery. Make your fortress forgettable. Keep a low profile, and the Adventurers will assume that you're not exciting. Don't give Adventurers any reason to think that throwing themselves into your path would be enjoyable. It's not foolproof protection, but it goes a long way towards safeguarding your interests.

And don't think you're safe from the Adventurers if you're a one-man operation. Large scale villains do attract more Adventurers, but small scale villains aren't immune. Simply being an outsider or a loner can be enough to draw their attention if they think tangling with you and your things will get them the thrill they seek.

I knew a giant by the name of Humphrey who had a comfortable life in a castle he purchased from a fairy. Built among the clouds, Humphrey thought it the perfect escape from the heroic persecution of trolls, giants, and ogres with the accompanying gruesome and bloody results. Unfortunately, he didn't count on some kid getting his hands on magic seeds that grew beanstalks high enough to reach his home right when it was passing over the lad's farm. Sadly enough, what comes next is not an uncommon occurrence; giants have a natural affinity for attracting Adventurers.

The boy climbed the beanstalk and found Humphrey's castle in the clouds. Perhaps he wouldn't have bothered if it had been just some normal home in a normal location, but I guess we'll never know.

Rather than knocking like a normal, polite person, the boy broke into Humphrey's home and took some gold. Personally, I'd call that breaking and entering, but laws don't apply to the Adventurer like they do to us mere mortals. As if that weren't bad enough, the thief came back more times, taking anything he could carry. Every time Humphrey tried to stop him, the kid skittered away like a cockroach.

The final time, Humphrey spotted the kid and chased him down the beanstalk. The kid reached the bottom with enough time to take an axe to it, felling the beanstalk and poor Humphrey with it. To this day, I can't stop the anger I feel at his death. Humphrey was neither villain nor hero. He wanted to live his life, quiet and happy. And he did until an Adventurer crossed his path.

The criminal lived high on the hog with what he stole

from Humphrey. He loved to tell the tale about the giant who threatened, "I'll grind his bones to make my bread" or some such nonsense. As if bones can be made into bread. But I guess, "I'll press criminal charges" doesn't have the same lyrical ring to it.

However, I did hear that the kid met with a string of bad luck. Some Punisher got his hooks into the boy. I won't disclose all the details, but though the lad is alive and well, he won't be Adventuring any time soon.

There's not much advice I can give you about how to deal with Adventurers because they are indiscriminate in where they go and what draws them into your life. The best I can say is try to fly under the radar. If you're uninteresting enough to draw the attention of the average person, you won't draw the attention of an Adventurer.

The Reluctant

Heroes won't jump into the action unless it benefits them in some way. For the Rescuer, it's the promise of getting the girl. For the Adventurer, it's the thrill. For the Reluctant, it's reversing a curse. Where other heroes may see the opportunity and jump into the fray, the Reluctant is only there because the villain threw him into it; if it weren't for the fairy/wizard/enchantress who cursed him, the guy would be sitting at home.

Reluctants are mostly princes because the majority are created by Havockers. True Havockers do it for the fun, and princes are an obnoxious group who deserve a little tormenting; paupers already have difficult lives and causing them more pain just isn't fun. Contracted Havockers do so for the money, which paupers can't pay.

There are occasional pauper Reluctants created by Punishers or out of control Overlords, such as an evil stepmother cursing her stepson either to punish or get him out of the way. But paupers are a minority among Reluctants. If you're looking to create one, you may want to go back and reread this manual again and reevaluate the motivations behind your actions; pauper Reluctants are indicative of personal issues.

Prince Reluctants are the most harmless heroes. If you pay attention to the principles already outlined (specifically "The Havocker" and "The Entrepreneur" sections of Chapter One), they won't be an issue. Curse and vacate the area, and the Reluctant Hero will go about the business of getting himself uncursed. No muss, no fuss. Remember: the Havocker who stays will be destroyed by the Reluctant. But this is all beside the point as I'm talking about the Reluctant, not the Havocker.

I heard about a Reluctant Hero a few years ago who had to be one of the most extreme examples I've come across. Like I mentioned before, Reluctants are lazy. Some may use the curse to spur them into action, but many sit back and let the heroine break it for them. A princeling who is too lazy to step outside his front door to Rescue generally won't muster the energy to fix his problems if there are others to do so.

In this case, this prince took the word idle to a whole new level. He was a young prince with a reputation for being a self-absorbed brat. I don't know what he did to earn such distinction. All princes are spoiled and teens are even worse; mix them together and you've got hell on earth for everyone around them. Regardless, he was a beastly kid.

A Havocker friend of mine crossed his path a few years

ago. Yvette needed shelter during a winter storm and went knocking on the door of the prince's castle. Normally, people welcome fairies with open arms, but the prince took one look at her and tossed her back into the cold with some not so kind comments about her looks. Needless to say, that didn't go over well with Yvette, and she cursed him to be ugly. Majorly ugly. Like people gasping and babies crying when they see him ugly.

She knew the prince would break the curse eventually—they all do—but the high level of hideousness guaranteed it would take a while before any heroine would take pity on him. But Yvette underestimated just how Reluctant he was.

Rather than setting off into the wide world to search for a girl to break the spell, the guy locked himself away in his castle and did nothing while the years ticked by. The kid was such an extreme Reluctant that even getting cursed wasn't enough motivation to shift his lazy carcass.

In the end, the prince never went in search for a girl. He extorted one from a poor, hapless traveler who plucked a rose from the castle's gardens. Cursing wasn't enough to encourage action, but stealing royal property was something the prince wouldn't stand for. Capturing the traveler, the prince demanded compensation for the stolen bloom, and the traveler offered up his youngest daughter.

I've heard people speak of this story with hushed whispers, claiming the goodness of the daughter drove her to sacrifice her freedom for her father's, but that's not true. Parents are quick to sacrifice their children to save themselves. The daughter no more volunteered to be a prisoner than the prince volunteered to be a monster.

The prince accepted, and the traveler delivered the future bride to the kid's door. The rest of the story continues on in the same vein. The prince did nothing but sit back and let the girl work herself into a romantic frenzy about the brooding beast she lived with. I don't understand the female inclination towards brooding men. At best, he ignore her. At worse, he's mean. It makes no sense, but it's like flies to honey. As in the flies land get stuck on the honey and slowly drown.

They say the prince allowed the girl to visit her family, but while she was gone his heart broke. She returned to find him dying, and her love healed him while breaking the curse. And they lived happily ever after.

But that's all a bunch of dragon dung the prince's wife likes to tell people. It sounds much better than His Lazy Highness did nothing to woo her; she did all the work in the relationship, and that didn't change after they married.

Though generally not dangerous to your health, Reluctants can harm the financial survival of contracted Havockers. If you're hired to curse a prince, it's because his frustrated parents are hoping to get him off his royal bum. Before you take on a client, make sure your Reluctant will do something to break the curse.

Cursing him may be the only thing listed in your contract, but the royals will expect that curse to end well for their beloved prince. Meaning, he needs to get the curse reversed and find his bride. If he doesn't, the parents won't think to blame him. They'll blame you. Either your reputation will be ruined or you'll be forced to step in and do extra work to get him to the finish line. Neither is a good outcome.

Yvette was a regular Havocker, so it didn't matter how lazy the Reluctant was. It wouldn't damage her villainous goals. If Yvette had been a contracted Havocker, the years it took her Reluctant to break the curse would have been filled with countless complaints from his parents, demanding something be done. Unhappy clients do a lot of damage to your reputation. Those happy with your work occasionally pass on the good news to other potential clients, but the unhappy ones will tell every living soul just how terrible you are at your job.

Luckily, this issue is mitigated with a cursory amount of research into your client before agreeing to any contract.

The Survivor

The Survivor is the rarest hero type. At first glance, they may not seem dangerous or problematic, but villains beware. The Survivor is fighting for his life, and that usually comes at the price of yours. They're vicious and unscrupulous. They will do anything to win, and they tend to burn a swath of destruction in their quest for survival.

The most difficult aspect of the Survivor is that they're children. They look sweet and innocent, but they're black to the core. If you turn your back on them for a second, they will do terrible things to you.

The Survivors are paupers of the lowest ranks, such as the children of woodcutters or farmers. Their parents raise them up until the day they decide the kids cost too much and abandon them in the woods. They simply march the children out into the woods until they're lost and leave them. It happens regularly enough that many pauper children refuse to go anywhere with their parents unless they're carrying a pouch of stones to trail behind them in order to find their way back home.

And they call us villains.

These children are scrappy. They've been raised in families where abandoning their kids in the woods is a valid form of budgeting. Such immoral parents are bound to have hellions for children who would slit your throat in your sleep.

You may think I'm exaggerating, but I've seen what Survivors can do. My friend, Elsa, was a gifted architect, she was my go-to contractor for designing office spaces and fortresses. She loved making mundane building supplies take on new life by designing them to appear like things you wouldn't expect.

Her own home was a masterpiece. She built the entire house to look like it was made of gingerbread and candy. I once asked her why she chose such a fanciful design, and though she wouldn't give me the entire story, she said it had to do with a favorite childhood memory.

Built in the deepest part of the forest, Elsa had a haven away from the squabbles of neighbors and angry townsfolk. It's appalling how often my contractors or employees are forced to move towns because the townsfolk don't want "our kind" around, even if they've never done anything villainous. Like Elsa. She was no villain.

One day, Elsa heard strange noises along the siding of her home and discovered two children prying off bits of gumdrops and icing. At first, she tried my suggested Survivor solution—scare the crap out of the kids and send them running—but the kids turned their big eyes up at Elsa and wore away her common sense.

When they explained their parents had abandoned them in the woods not once but twice, Elsa's heart was lost. I tried to talk some sense into her when she told me what was going on, but she was too sentimental for her own good.

It sounded as though things went well for a while, but when Elsa didn't show up for a meeting, I went to investigate and found her remains burning in her stove. The kids had the gall to show up later with their parents in tow to claim Elsa's home and possessions as compensation for her trying to kill them. Elsa, now called "The Witch" by these "innocent" children, was accused of attempted cannibalism. The more likely story is that they saw an opportunity to get a well-furnished house and a mountain of savings she'd amassed.

I have seen and heard a lot of horrifying things in my life, but I can tell you that nothing has come close to what these kids did to Elsa. She never hurt anyone in her life. She wasn't a witch and didn't rely on stray children to supplement her diet.

Watching them swoop in and rearrange her home to suit their needs while the smell of burnt flesh still hung in the air chilled me to my core. These Survivors didn't bat an eye at burning a poor innocent woman alive. I have no idea what led them to that point, but I know Elsa was innocent.

Luckily, their good fortune was short-lived. A Punisher got hold of them and saw justice done. The family ended up accused of a different crime (killing a witch isn't one, after all). Despite their insistence of innocence, mountains of evidence pointed to them, and they are currently serving the rest of their lives in prison.

Survivors are the worst of all the heroes because they slip right past your defenses and can be more cruel and vile than any of the others. Do not let yourself be taken in by them. If you meet a child lost in the woods or abandoned, let it be. Even if you think this one will be different, don't! The more pathetic and innocent they look, the more likely they are to destroy you when your defenses are down.

Especially brother and sister duos. They're doubly dangerous. While heroines have their own separate category, the Survivor is hazier when it comes to gender. A single Survivor will always be a boy, but it's not uncommon to find them in pairs. In which case, one will be a girl.

The Mercenary

Money isn't a core motivator for heroes. Ever. Anyone chasing money is considered a villain. The Entrepreneur villain exists because the powers that be consider it gauche for money to be the impetus behind heroic actions.

The Mercenary isn't a pure type of hero, but rather a subset. Where the Mercenary comes in is after the heroic journey has started. If riches are stumbled upon by a hero, they're fair game to steal. In Humphrey's case, he faced an Adventurer who was there for the sole purpose of having an interesting story to tell, but the minute the kid saw Humphrey's riches, he focused on the gold and only the gold. Or Elsa's case. The kids started off as Survivors, fighting for their lives but switched when a chance for more substantial gain presented itself.

Once the hero has stepped foot out the door for any reason other than money, all bets are off.

And as a side note, I would say that although I'm talking about money, it can include any plunder the hero desires. Once they've made an attempt to do their heroic job, they'll want to claim rewards they may or may not have earned. Fair warning to all those looking to use their daughters as royalty bait—Rescuers are not always single, but all expect an amorous reward, even if they can't promise marriage.

There's not a lot of advice to be given when it comes to this subset other than the usual things when dealing with robbers. Keep your valuables out of sight of strangers and watch your wallet. And your life.

The only other piece of advice is that if you have a Mercenary infestation, either get better security or let them take your things. Chasing after a Mercenary guarantees your death. When it comes to heroes invading your home in any way, shape, or form, the best course of action is to move. If a hero stumbles across your doorstep don't fight him, just move.

Chapter Ten

Heroines

I'm not going to go as in depth about heroines as I am about heroes, as they're not as important. Generally, they do little to nothing to hurt you. Even if you've ignored my previous advice and included a heroine in your villainous goals, the heroine will do nothing to ruin them. They're not the problem—it's the hero who comes after her.

Heroines are similar to heroes in that they have two classes: the princess and the pauper. The heroic and magic status quo have no interest in those in the middle.

In order for a pauper to become a heroine, she must be breathtakingly beautiful as well as selflessly kind. Or at least, the magical element call it kindness, but more often than not, the "kindness" their describing is more like being a docile doormat. Magical helpers

As a side note, if you have a gorgeous daughter, ship her off to live in a dump somewhere in the woods. Make her a pauper heroine and wait for a prince or king to stroll by. You'd be astonished how often this happens. For one thing, Rescuers often tend to wander the woods in search of someone to save and are easily reeled in if they see a pretty enough face. It's like trolling for royalty.

The Damsel in Distress

The Damsel in Distress (or DID) constitutes almost the entirety of heroines. Like the Reluctant Hero, DIDs tend to sit back and wait for life to happen to them. They don't take control of their story, but that is due to docility rather than the Reluctant's laziness. DIDs get cursed or kidnapped or forced into an engagement by some stupid villain, and the Rescuer shows up and saves the day. DIDs don't do anything, unless you count pricking your finger on a spindle or biting an apple as doing something.

Charles's daughter is a prime example of this, and she used her passivity to his betterment (see "The Counselor" section in Chapter One). When he left his daughter in the care of the wicked stepmother, he knew it wouldn't take long before the stepmother had his daughter deep into servitude.

Pathetically enough, it took less time than we anticipated. The girl never questioned what was happening. There was no fighting or fuss. She accepted the hardship without question. I'd dealt with a DID here and there before, but this was the first time I saw up close and personal how passive they truly are.

The most extreme case I've heard of was a woman by the name of Zelda. She was living in a home in the middle of the forest when a prince wandered by and was so taken by her beauty, he instantly fell in "love". That's what they always claim, but let's face it, it wasn't love that caught the guy's eye. But either way, he married her and took her home, only to decide he didn't trust her. Her being a stranger he'd just picked up in the woods wasn't so much the issue, but the fact that she was a woman.

For the first fifteen years of their marriage, the guy tormented Zelda, trying to "test" her. He claimed it was to see if she would remain true to him, but really, he wanted to see if his dear little wife was unquestioningly obedient to his every whim.

It started small. He demanded Zelda give up her possessions. Everything he gave to her, he'd eventually ask for back. Then their first child was born. Her husband told Zelda she'd never be fit to raise their daughter to be a proper princess. I would have given him a good punch to the face, but Zelda just gave him the baby. Just to rub salt into the wound, he told her a few days later the baby had died. Zelda mourned, but never raised a fuss about the situation.

The same happened with their second baby.

As if that wasn't bad enough, the guy went a step further. He abandoned Zelda, sending her back to her old cottage, claiming her low birth disqualified her from being his wife. He was about to ascend the throne and needed a royal bride by his side. Again, Zelda did nothing but wish him well.

At this point, I'm not sure if the gal had all her faculties intact because her actions were beyond bizarre. I know the power violence has in keeping people, but the prince never stooped so low as to threaten her. He simply asked and Zelda gave.

When the wedding day came and Zelda was still perfectly supportive, the prince/new king decided she'd been tested enough and had proven herself the ideal spineless wife for him. He told Zelda it had all been a lie; he wasn't marrying someone else and their two children were alive. The king reintroduced Zelda to their now teenaged kids, and true to form, Zelda not only accepted this, but welcomed her kids and husband with open arms.

This is an extreme example. Obviously, both the prince/king and Zelda were a bit off-kilter and might not be a great example, but heroines tend towards a high level of passive acceptance. They don't kick up a fuss, so they don't cause problems for most villains by themselves.

In rare cases DIDs will take action. In the case of imminent demise or incest (that is an actual problem that crops up from time to time among the royalty), a DID will run for it, but she generally throws herself on the mercy of others to protect her. But the running doesn't generally cause problems unless your plans involve keeping your hands on the heroine. Just let them go, and you'll be fine.

But I will repeat myself one more time: do not involve heroines in your plans if you can help it! Leave them be.

The Wanderer

The heroine meets the hero and falls in "love" with him, and everyone expects them to ride off into the sunset to get their happily ever after. But that doesn't always happen. Occasionally, circumstances separate the couple, creating the Wanderer.

If an incident separates them after the hero has done his heroic deed and gotten the girl, he will do nothing more to reunite with her. I don't understand the psychology behind it nor do I want to, but more often than not, the heroics are then placed on the heroine's shoulders. The heroine will set off on some grand quest, wandering the world in search of her prince, and the prince won't do anything until she shows up.

In most situations, the Wanderer is only a problem if you're holding onto her prince. If you're the one who kidnapped the guy, the Wanderer will find you, free the hero, and your days will be numbered. As long as you don't hold on to her hero, you will never have a problem from the Wanderer.

Unlike the Adventurer who cuts a path of destruction wherever he goes, the Wanderer doesn't cause a fuss while she's looking for her hero. She tends to get random blessings from kindly fairies or other magical creatures who guide her to her prince, or she simply walks and walks until she finds him. Either way, she's not like some of the heroes who cause problems all along the way.

One of my clients, Brigitta, was a perpetual headache. She had the hardest time understanding how to work with heroes and heroines. And choosing a villainy path. And sticking to her goals. And many other things. She was a complete mess that I should have never taken on in the first place, but I couldn't help myself. Some clients get under my skin, and it's hard to cut them loose.

Brigitta was exceptionally unattractive. Not non-beautiful, but full on ugly. So ugly, in fact, that many people called her a troll, which is monstrously unfair. I've seen trolls, and Brigitta wasn't even near that level of disgusting, but that is beside the point. The point is that she was ugly enough that she had no hopes for the future.

Her family made a decent enough living, but as the youngest of seven, Brigitta had little hope of receiving any inheritance, and when people refer to you as a troll, there's little hope of finding a husband and building a home of your own. Brigitta even tried finding a job for herself to earn her own money, but as I mentioned at various times in this guide, people equate beautiful with good and ugly with bad, so it makes it difficult to find work when people think you're some malevolent troll wanting to eat their children.

Which left her with only one option: villainy.

I was able to find her an internship with a Havocker, as it seemed the best education for her. Though she wasn't raised learning magic, she developed a knack for it and proved herself to be a decent enchantress. It was exciting to see her develop her skills and eventually grow in prestige enough to strike out on her own as a contracted Havocker.

She took a job cursing a prince from a kingdom to the north, but she made the mistake of meeting the guy first. Brigitta liked a hands-on approach to her curses, including meeting the future accursed to tailor the spell for them. Most of the time this wasn't a problem, but this prince was her Achilles heel, and she fell head over heels for the guy. I never understood her obsession with him, but I think too many years of being treated unkindly by others left her vulnerable to any kindness. All it took was a couple smiles and a kind word or two, and she was a goner. I will admit, I was surprised that any prince would take the time to be halfway decent to a random stranger, but there are always outliers.

She cursed him to take the form of a bear. Brigitta knew that would scare off most heroines, leaving Brigitta a chance to break the curse herself, giving her an automatic engagement. However, the prince figured out what she wanted and ran for it. Again, most heroes would simply kill Brigitta and break the curse that way, but as I said moments ago, he's an outlier.

He befriended some peasant girl and bribed the girl's parents to send her off to live with him in his cave, hoping that if the girl spent time with him, she'd fall in love and break the curse.

When Brigitta caught up with him and found the girl there, she was furious and stole the prince away, sending him to her fortress far off to the east. Brigitta turned him back into a man, but enchanted him to fall in love with her and forget the other girl. That was enough of a mistake, but she took it one step further.

The heroine went in search of her hero. With a healthy dose of magical help, she eventually found her way to Brigit's fortress. If at any time Brigitta had released the hero and moved on with her life, it would have been fine. I warned Brigitta to let the prince go, but at this point, Brigitta believed it was too late to back out.

Confident she had the prince perfectly ensorcelled, Brigitta taunted the heroine. She let the heroine bribe her with a trinket in exchange for a visit with the hero. The heroine thought seeing him would be enough to break the enchantment, but when the heroine was brought to her prince, she found him drugged and unconscious. Realizing she was so near yet unable to save him broke her heart.

Brigitta enjoyed tricking the heroine so much that she did it another time. Unable to keep her pride in check, she did so a third time, but by this time, the prince was aware enough to realize something was going on. When Brigitta brought the sleeping draught to the prince, he tricked Brigitta into thinking he'd drunk it.

There was way too much tricking going on.

The prince pretended to sleep. Brigitta left. The heroine came in. The prince opened his eyes. Their kiss broke the enchantment. They escaped. And Brigitta got crushed under the wreckage of her castle when the prince and his fiancé decided to bring it down on their way out.

The Wanderer may constitute a small percentage of heroines but be wary of her. Not because she's particularly strong, but if she gets the hero to wriggle out of your imprisonments, you'll be in serious trouble.

The Sister

Where the DID is completely inactive, the Wanderer and Sister both actively work to undo your plans—the Wanderer because you stole their prince and the Sister because you cursed her brother. Like I mentioned before, some Reluctants use that kick in the pants to get them moving. However, at other times the Reluctant is willing to sit back and let others break the curse for them. The Sister is a heroine with a cursed brother who shows no interest in fixing the curse himself or cannot do so, leaving his dear Sister to save the day.

The Sister differs from a Survivor in that she is alone in her fight to fix things (meaning the brother is doing nothing to help the situation). Where the Survivor is fighting for her and her brother to survive, the Sister is saving her brother from an enchantment.

I knew a woman by the name of Katelyn with royal aspirations. She wanted to be a Counselor but was far too driven by sentimentality to be successful. I tried working with her, but Katelyn proved unfocused.

After we cancelled our contract, Katelyn went on to find a modicum of success by tricking a king into marrying her. Extortion can work well in many instances, but when used for marriage, it tends to cause nothing but problems. Eventually, the king became too hard to control, so Katelyn arranged for an "accident" to get him out of the way and focused on manipulating her stepson, the crown prince.

But every royal mother knows bachelor kings eventually marry and put the old queen into storage. This particular stepson/king was wandering the woods and found a gorgeous, mute girl and fell instantly in love with her as royal are wont to do. Frankly, Katelyn should have left it alone. The girl couldn't talk. She wasn't causing any problems or usurping Katelyn's role as Counselor to the king. But like I mentioned before, rational thought wasn't Katelyn's forte.

After their first baby was born, Katelyn stole the child and hid it in the forest, making it look like the new queen had murdered and eaten the baby. You might think it was overkill to throw in a bit of cannibalism, but then you'd be underestimating just how attractive the new queen was.

The king refused to accept the evidence because he knew his wife was pure and virtuous. How he understood that is a mystery. The woman never spoke, wrote, or gestured a single word. But then again, she was exceptionally stunning. That's generally all the proof royals need.

He still didn't accept the evidence when their second child met the same fate.

With the third one, the king finally capitulated and sentenced the queen to be burned at the stake.

When that happened, Katelyn crowed over me and my foolish decision to cut her loose. She felt secure and happy in the knowledge that her plan had worked. Never mind that things weren't over yet and it would only repeat itself when the prince remarried, but again, the logic wasn't working for Katelyn.

And she didn't know her stepdaughter-in-law was really a Sister.

Before being a random pretty girl in the forest, the queen was a princess from a neighboring kingdom. Her evil stepmother had cursed the heroine's brothers to turn into swans. The heroine had escaped and figured out that weaving shirts from some outlandish material combined with not speaking for seven years would save her brothers from their swanish fate.

I can absolutely, without a doubt, guarantee that if there's a time limit on a curse, it will end at the exact moment a villain "wins". Especially if that is timed with the hero's or heroine's death. Everything will come together in some impossibly perfect combination to save them and destroy you. Which is what happened to Katelyn.

The mute queen had almost finished the shirts when the day of her execution arrived. She even carried them with her to the pyre, working on the final sleeve as she marched to her death. Katelyn should have been paying attention; if you see a heroine feverishly working on some mysterious project, especially at an odd time (like her execution), you can bet that you have a Sister on your hands trying to break some curse.

The flames rose, and the heroine threw the shirts into the air. The brothers/swans swooped down and slid them on, transforming back into their human selves, except for one brother's wing that had been sticking out under the unfinished sleeve. At that point, the queen was free to speak and told the king everything Katelyn had done.

Guess who ended up on the pyre that day?

If Katelyn had watched for the signs and realized what she was up against, she could have adjusted her plans towards a more favorable outcome. By simply abandoning the silly baby-snatching and treating her new stepdaughter-in-law kindly, Katelyn would have lost her Counselor role but kept her life.

Chapter Eleven

The Hero Myth

Heroes are treated with far too much reverence. They're humans, like you and I, and more flawed than most give them credit for. Though heroes would lead people to believe they're the epitome of perfection, that's just their overinflated egos talking.

Myth #1: Heroes are altruistic

Heroes are painted as self-sacrificing do-gooders, but that is patently false. No hero, whether high or lowborn, steps foot out the door without an ulterior motive. Even the Rescuer, who is viewed as the most altruistic of the heroes, is only in it to get the girl. They won't lift a finger if it doesn't further their agenda.

I knew a young lady by the name of Adriana. She'd been trapped in a sleeping spell for so long that none of her family or friends were alive when she finally awoke. Her father was lord of the manor, and it had been foretold at her birth that she would fall asleep after she got a splinter of flax lodged in her finger. Strange, I know.

Her father shipped her body off to one of his country estates, and there she lay for many years until a king stumbled across her path. I've heard this story told many times, and each time, the heroism and goodness of the king is described in great length, but it's hard for me to see that after hearing the rest of the story.

He tried to wake her as any good hero would do. However, when she remained asleep, his Rescuer façade dropped and the Mercenary took over; he saw what he wanted, and when she wouldn't give it to him willingly, he simply forced himself on her. The man was already married, after all, so there wouldn't have been wedding bells in Adriana's future whether or not he woke her.

When finished, the king returned home to his wife, but returned to Adriana's comatose bed from time to time. Eventually she gave birth to a set of twins. Since he couldn't explain to his wife where the babies came from, he left them with the still sleeping Adriana, not caring what happened to them.

Eventually, the splinter of flax worked its way out of her finger, and Adriana awoke to find herself the proud momma of two sickly babies with her Rescuer nowhere in sight. As there were only three people in that room, and none of them could tell what was going on at the time, I suppose we'll never know for certain how the flax got out, though the prevailing theory is that one of the babies sucked it out of her finger.

To his surprise, when the king arrived looking to indulge himself, he found himself with a conscious heroine and two squalling children. Eventually, his wife found out and there was a bit more drama, but that's not particularly important to the point I'm trying to make.

Do not buy into the saintly demeanor many of the heroes affect. People view them as paragons, but they're as human as everybody else. With the royals, they're often even more selfish than the average person.

Myth #2: Heroes will come after villains no matter what

As I said previously, heroes are only in this for their own purposes. If your plans do not intersect with theirs, they won't bother you. Even if they do, if you're not there when Judgment Day arrives, they won't come after you. Basically, unless you are standing directly in front of them, they'll leave you alone. Period.

But as a lot of villains have issues with vanity and enjoy the spotlight too much, they often hang around for much longer than they should. Or they resort to childish antics to bask in the glory of their perceived victory and taunt the hero or heroine before leaving.

Look at Brigitta's example from the previous chapter (see "The Wanderer" section). Brigitta did so many things wrong during her last job that it's hard to point to a specific moral in her story. It was a good example of how falling in love can destroy you, but what ultimately did her in was the fact that she misunderstood how heroes and heroines work. No matter what you do to them, heroes will not bother themselves with hunting you down unless you take a prince away from his heroine or vice versa.

If Brigitta had walked away the minute the heroine showed up, she would still be alive. Once he was taken, she not only indulged in too much pride, but fell prey to the misbelief that once she moved past a certain point with the hero and heroine, there was no backing out. But that is simply not true.

You can walk away at any point. As long as you're not there when the hero and heroine are reunited, you will be fine. Heroes only look out for their own interests and care little about tracking you down once they have what they want.

Myth #3: Heroes are honest

This pervasive myth is a detriment to the Entrepreneur. As much of their villainy is tied to making deals with heroes and heroines, they are often defeated because they believe heroes stick to their deals.

However, heroes prove time and again that they

cannot be trusted. You are a villain. Thus, in their mind, any deal they make with you is automatically invalid. Though some have no honor and break their word the moment it's spoken, most use technicalities and loopholes. They do not view such as cheating, so they can live their honorable lives, secure and happy in the knowledge that they lived up to the agreement.

I've shared enough examples of this I shouldn't have to illustrate it further. If you need a refresher, please go back and read about Wilhelm (see "The Entrepreneur" section of Chapter One) or Tom (see the "Morality and Conscience" section of Chapter Three).

Villains are universally believed to be cheats and liars, but heroes are the true thieves. Besides the fact that many of them are simply conmen who will rob you blind, they have no compunction in wiggling out of a deal. Be careful.

Myth #4: Heroes are kind

You only need to worry about this if your plans fall apart and you're forced into facing the hero. Notice that I say forced. There is no reason for you to seek out the hero. As I've said before, avoid them when possible, but there are times when that's not an option. In that moment, you can't count on the hero to be kind.

Generally, I'm a proponent of having backup plans. And backup plans of backup plans. However, when fighting a hero, if you fail, there are only two options left: beg for mercy or fall on your sword. Heroes can be kind and merciful. If you beg for mercy, some heroes will automatically forgive and forget what you did, no matter how bad. They can be insanely trusting at times, but what you need to be aware of is that there is another very likely scenario that will play out—your gruesomely over-the-top execution.

You may have done some wicked things in pursuit of your goals, but what heroes do in retaliation will pale in comparison. Once you cross the line into villainy, heroes view that as a free pass to do all the vile things their heart wishes. Attempted murderers are fitted with red-hot iron shoes and forced to dance until they die or are thrown into pits full of venomous creepy-crawlies. Tradesmen are drawn and quartered for asking a price deemed too high. Putting a temporary curse on someone gives them license to burn people at the stake.

If faced with relying on the goodness of the hero to live, you're better off falling on your own sword. Yes, there are some who would grant you a pardon, but the chances of a grisly death is far more likely.

Adela was a client of mine (notice the past tense), smart enough to be dangerous and pretty enough to turn heads. As a handmaiden to her country's princess, she lived within touching distance of wealth, opulence, and power but had none of it for herself.

The princess had everything she wanted except an interest in the responsibility that came with all the pomp and circumstance of royal life. When her parents arranged her marriage to the prince of a faraway kingdom, the princess threw a fit. She complained to anyone who would listen about her agonizing lot in life; she was convinced that peasants had it far better, and Adela saw her chance.

She approached the princess and offered to trade places. Adela would marry the far away prince and the real princess would be provided with the resources to have the quiet life of which she always dreamed. The princess grabbed the offer with both hands and praised Adela for sacrificing her freedom. It really was a beautifully simple plan, and one that required little effort since the princess was on board with it.

However, while many royals have the misconception that their life has less freedom than non-royals, the truth is that absolute freedom is a myth. Everyone has responsibilities, obligations, and limitations, and changing your situation doesn't get rid of that. As the princess soon discovered.

Once outside the view of her people, the princess switched places with Adela. They paid off their guards, and the princess was settled in a comfortable situation with a sizable settlement far from her home country and the kingdom of Adela's prince-to-be.

All seemed wonderful, and Adela had an uneventful rise to prominence in her new home as the future queen. But the freedom the real princess sought wasn't as free as she had dreamed, and she soon got tired of the rustic lifestyle. She no longer had to attend the endless functions and perform the mindless royal duties, but she also no longer had people bowing and scraping to curry her favor or new silk gowns every week or lavish parties every fortnight.

After a few months of "endless torture" (the princess's words, not mine), she decided marriage to a complete stranger wasn't as bad as she had envisioned and headed off to find Adela and switch back. At that point, I would have advised Adela to acquiesce, but she didn't want to go to Plan B after everything was going so well. And she overestimated the relationship she and the prince had formed during their time together.

When it was proved that Adela was an imposter, her loving prince sentenced her to death. Her husband-to-be, future in-laws, and business partner stripped her naked, threw her into a barrel full of glass shards and nails, and dragged it through the streets.

Heroes pretend to be virtuous and kind, but they're more bloodthirsty than any villain with whom I've ever worked. They wrap themselves in piety but will torture and mutilate you without a second thought. Heroes dole out punishments far greater than the crime. Do not overestimate the amount of mercy they have. Without hesitation, they will play judge, jury, and executioner. And torturer.

A Word Before We Go

I hope you find this guide useful in your villainous preparations. Though not everything outlined here will apply to you, there are kernels of truth in every section that can help you achieve the success you wish for. As I said in the beginning of this book, your success relies on knowledge and how well you apply it. Heroes stack the deck in their favor, and the only real weapon you have on your side is that knowledge. Hopefully, I've been able to add to it and give you enough guidance and understanding to help you make wise decisions.

It's important to remember that all things come to an end. No matter your plans, inevitably, they will end. Even if you succeed in getting everything you want, eventually, you will die and your plans will cease to exist. You will no longer be king or queen, you will no longer have that pile of money you've collected, you will no longer be the best or brightest.

It will fade away as you move onto the next sphere of existence. The key is to make sure that you live your life the best that you can. Revel in your successes and learn from your mistakes.

Remember that being a villain isn't some awful thing. Villain is a word that means different things to different people. To a prince, it's a demon. To a princess, the catalyst for change. To the pauper, a hurdle to jump. To me, it's merely someone who tries to choose their own path in life. Villains aren't villainous, and heroes aren't heroic. If nothing else, I hope that you've had your eyes opened to the possibility of what your future can hold. Don't accept the lot you've been given. Strive to better your circumstances.

Being villainous is not a matter of being evil. It's a matter of perspective.

Geoffrey R. Ward

About the Author

Born and raised in Anchorage, M.A. Nichols is a lifelong Alaskan with a love of the outdoors. As a child she despised reading but through the love and persistence of her mother was taught the error of her ways and has had a deep, abiding relationship with it ever since.

She graduated with a bachelor's degree in landscape management from Brigham Young University and a master's in landscape architecture from Utah State University, neither of which has anything to do with why she became a writer, but is a fun little tidbit none-the-less. And no, she doesn't have any idea what type of plant you should put in that shady spot out by your deck. She's not that kind of landscape architect. Stop asking.

For more information about M.A. Nichols and her books visit her webpage at www.ma-nichols.com or check out her Goodreads page (www.goodreads.com/manichols). For up to date information and news, visit her Facebook page (www.facebook.com/manicholsauthor).

Books by M.A. Nichols

The Tréaltha Series

The Drogue
The Rinaldi Triplets: A Novella
Blood of the Warden
The First Great War: A Novella

Exclusive Offer

Join the M.A. Nichols VIP Reader Club at
www.ma-nichols.com
to receive up-to-date information and exclusive offers!

One More Thing

Thank you for reading *Geoffrey P. Ward's Guide to Villainy*!
If you enjoyed it, please write a review on Amazon and
Goodreads and help us spread the word.

88196754R00095

Made in the USA
Columbia, SC
01 February 2018